Advanced Combat Magic

Ember Academy for Young Witches, Volume 5

L.C. Mawson

Published by L.C. Mawson, 2020.

This is a work of fiction. Similarities to real people, places, or events are entirely coincidental.

ADVANCED COMBAT MAGIC

First edition. July 9, 2020.

Written by L.C. Mawson.

Also by L.C. Mawson

Engineered Magic
Soulbound

Engineered Rebel
Rebel
Resist
Rebuild
Reconnect
Reconsider
Resolution

Freya Snow
Hunt
White
Wings
Oracle
Witch
Enhanced
Reaper
Trident
Kingsguard
Princess
Queen
Warden
Pandora

Sacrifice
Darkness
Trapped
The Freya Snow Pup Trilogy: Books 1-3
Freya Snow Short Story Collection
The Freya Snow Hammer Trilogy: Books 4-6
Freya Snow - The Beginning: Books 1-6
The Freya Snow Elemental Trilogy: Books 7-9
The Freya Snow Princess Trilogy: Books 10-12
The Freya Snow Final Trilogy: Books 13-15
Freya Snow: The End (Books 7-15)
The Freya Snow Complete Collection (Books One to Fifteen)

The Almosts Trilogy
The Almosts
The Damned
The Almosts: The Complete Trilogy
The Redeemed

The Lady Ruth Constance Chapelstone Chronicles
Lady Ruth Constance Chapelstone and the Clockwork Suitor
Lady Ruth Constance Chapelstone and the Parisian Thief
Lady Ruth Constance Chapelstone and the American Escapade
The Complete Lady Ruth Constance Chapelstone Chronicles

The Royal Cleaner
Target
Home

Table of Contents

Thank you to all of my supporters for helping me fuel my new soap-making hobby.

Special thanks go out to Seph De Busser, Peter Allan and Jo Curnoe!

Cover by MoorBooks Design.

Chapter One

"Amy! Are you okay?"

I turned to my auntie as she and Ms Griffin ran up onto the wooden stage the Council had constructed.

The stage built for Maria's execution.

The stage that had now served its purpose...

"Amelia," Ms Griffin said when I didn't respond, placing a hand on my shoulder, "are you all right? Do you need to go to the infirmary? Are you injured?"

"I..." I failed to get any more words out, my throat tightening.

Auntie Jess stepped closer. "Did the Council do anything to you? Put you under a spell that needs lifting?"

My thoughts turned to static as I struggled to process their words.

"Okay," Freya said, gently pulling everyone back, giving me room to breathe. I sighed with relief as the aura of Nature surrounding her washed over me, calming my thoughts. "I think Amy needs some space. Maybe just one of us should take her somewhere quiet. I could-"

Then she stopped herself, turning to give me an apologetic smile. "Sorry. It's been so long... You probably need someone more familiar."

"No," I protested, finally finding my words at the thought of the soothing feel of nature radiating from my sister being taken away. "No, Freya, you... Connecting to elemental magic is helping right now."

Freya nodded in understanding. "Of course. Then I know just where to go."

She turned to Auntie Jess and Ms Griffin. "Assuming that's okay with you two."

They both hesitated, but then my auntie nodded. "Okay, Freya. Just... Let us know if you need anything."

Freya nodded before putting her arm around my shoulder, leading me away from the stage.

It took everything I had not to look back.

Not to finally see what remained of Maria.

"Where are we going?" I managed to ask, keeping my focus on Freya to avoid looking back.

"Somewhere safe. A haven of sorts."

I just nodded as she brought us to the edge of the woods.

And then we stepped through, only to step into Nature's clearing.

I looked around, frowning slightly. "Wait... The entrance to the clearing is deeper in the woods."

"The what?"

I turned back to Freya. "The entrance to Nature's clearing I usually use is deeper in the woods."

Freya smiled slightly. It didn't look real. It was the same smile Nature gave, the facsimile of Human interaction.

Still, I wasn't unnerved by it. No, her emotions fuelled her elemental magic, and I could sense that. So, while the smile looked fake, I knew that it was real.

"There is no specific entrance to the clearing. Nature just allows you through when you ask, and she wants to let you in. I thought she only allowed her Daughters through, but I suppose you must be close enough."

I nodded, the conversation acting as a useful distraction from...

Hot tears welled behind my eyes as I remembered again.

Freya responded by drawing me into her arms.

"It's okay, Amy. You're away from the Council now. They can't hurt you."

"But they already did," I blubbered against her armour.

She took a moment to ask, "Because they killed Maria?"

I nodded.

"She cut off our bond," I eventually said. "When Michael killed her... She cut me off from our bond so that I couldn't feel it. But that meant that she... She had no one *there* when she..."

Freya just held me tighter. "Shit, Amy, I am so sorry. Aaron mentioned that you were connected, but I... I can't imagine losing someone you're tethered to like that."

I couldn't formulate a response, sobs wracking my body as Freya just held me close, only gently moving me over to sit by one of the trees as the last of my strength left me.

Moments later, I passed out.

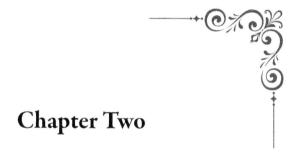

Chapter Two

I awoke groggily with a frown.

Why was I groggy? I was never normally groggy when I appeared in Maria's tower...

Except I wasn't in Maria's tower.

No, I'd only ever gone to her tower because she was there and I was tied to her.

But now, she was gone.

And I'd slept the whole night through, waking in the clearing where I'd fallen asleep.

Tears once more welled in my eyes at the realisation, the salt of last night's still clinging to my lips.

I tried to sense Maria, hoping for some spark of her through our bond.

Maybe I was wrong. Maybe this was all some trick of hers...

But no. I sensed nothing.

She was really gone.

A warmth spread from inside of me, correcting me.

She was gone, but her knowledge and her magic still lived on through the spell she'd cast.

Damn it, how long had she known that her death was likely? Had she been preparing for it when she'd cast that spell?

I failed to hold back the tears as Freya stirred beside me, also waking.

As soon as she saw that I was crying, she placed a gentle hand on my shoulder.

"You don't have to talk about it if you don't want to, Amy, but if you do, I'm here."

I nodded, not sure if I wanted to talk or not.

Not sure if I needed to get these thoughts from my head, or if saying them aloud would only make them more real.

And even if I did want to talk... Freya's elemental magic was familiar to me, but she was effectively a stranger.

Just because I remembered what she had been like before she'd left, didn't mean that I knew the woman she was now.

And even whom she had been in the past... I had been a small child. Who was to say that I had ever really known her?

She had suppressed both my memories of her and my magic, after all. Even if it had been dangerous for me to remember... How could she let me forget?

I pulled my knees up to my chest, hugging them close.

A moment later, there was a rustling noise in the bushes, and my head shot up as my hand went to my wand.

Was it the Council? Had they found us?

A large, white wolf padded from the bushes and I let out a breath of relief, loosening my grip on my wand.

Of course the Council hadn't found us here.

No one could get me here unless Nature allowed it.

"Nature," Freya greeted as the wolf approached. "Good morning. Thank you for letting us stay here last night."

The wolf bowed its head before pushing that same head between my chest and my knees, prying them apart.

"What-" I started, but as soon as my legs were down, the wolf flopped down on top of them like a large dog.

My hand went to scratch behind her ears without thought, and she didn't seem to object as the connection to her magic through her proximity acted like a wave of calm over me, settling my nerves as the last of my tears fell.

Freya smiled. "Nature doesn't always like people, but she seems to really like you. You know, Aaron told me about how you met her, but I wonder if he has the whole story. Or the whole story about anything."

I sighed, still not sure about talking. Though Nature's presence helped. The calm coming off her in waves focused my thoughts, and made me less unsure of what I wanted to say.

But still not sure that I wanted to say them to Freya.

I turned to her. She wanted to know about me, but I didn't want to open up before I figured her out.

"Why did you leave?" I asked. "When I was little, I mean. Auntie Jess explained, but I wonder if she has the whole story."

Freya sighed at me echoing her words back to her, tucking a loose strand of hair behind her ear. "I doubt it, given that I didn't have the full story at the time."

"Well, what was it? Why did you leave, and why did you take my memories?"

"The short answer is because my enemies found me, and it became too dangerous for me to stay with you."

"Auntie Jess explained that much, but you just made the Council of Light shit their pants. If you can do that, surely you could have protected us..."

Freya grimaced. "I can do that now, Amy. Back then... I wasn't as powerful. And I didn't understand how powerful I would become. At that point, I knew that my mother had been an Angel, but I had no idea who my father was. I'd figured out that I was half-Demon, but that was my only clue. The first Demon Queen gave her family powers beyond that of other Demons and I had no idea that I also had them at the time. So, yes, I could have ordered the Demons to back down and leave you and our parents alone, but I didn't even know that was a possibility.

"And my elemental abilities... They weren't as strong back then. I almost died a few years later and I only survived by shedding my humanity. It shifted my perception to be closer to Nature's, which made it easier for me to access my elemental powers. But that was later."

"So... You really couldn't stay?"

She shook her head. "I had the house protected under as many wards as possible, as strong as I could make them, yet the Demons still broke through. They had our parents at sword-point, and I barely managed to fight them off." She moved her hand to her abdomen. "I nearly didn't get away myself. If my best friend hadn't been a healer... Well, I might have been screwed.

"I didn't know exactly why they were after me at that point, but I knew that I threatened the power of a particularly nasty Demon Lord. Until I defeated him, I knew it wouldn't be safe for me to return home. For anyone to think that I still cared about the Human family I left behind."

I nodded, supposing that that did make sense.

I returned my attention to stroking Nature's fur.

I'd known that Freya must have had good reason to leave, but... Well, she'd been able to stand up to the Council. What if she'd been there earlier? What if she hadn't kept her distance?

But that was my fault as much as hers, I remembered, ice creeping up from the pit in my stomach. Mr Stiles had offered to take me to the Underworld, to stay safe under Freya's protection.

The Council wouldn't have been able to touch me, and Maria... Maria would have had no reason to step in to protect me.

But the Council would have taken that out on the school, taking away the one safe haven my friends had.

But had that been worth Maria's life? I'd put my own safety on the line, but Maria hadn't made that decision.

I'd made it for her.

I hadn't known that I was doing that at the time, but shouldn't I have?

Shouldn't I have known that if the Council put me in danger, Maria would try to save me?

But I hadn't, not until it was too late. Even when I was telling her to leave me be... I thought that would be enough.

And I'd been wrong.

I refocused, not sure what to do with that thought.

"Did you mean to suppress my magic along with my memories?" I asked Freya. "Auntie Jess was never quite sure."

Freya sighed. "No, I didn't. As I said, I didn't understand my powers at the time. I... I knew that you would be powerful, though I didn't know why. And you could already see through glamours without help. It was likely that you would break through early, probably when you were ten or eleven, and with Human parents... Well, hopefully Jess would have taken you to live with her, away from your parents, but if she couldn't... Well, the local coven would have taken you in, and probably erased your parents' memories of you. After the way I'd left, I wanted you to be old enough to decide how to handle things.

"Of course, that was just an errant thought on my part, I hadn't realised that I'd woven it into my magic."

"When did you realise?" I asked, wondering if she'd been keeping tabs on me as I'd grown up. If she'd thought about me at all...

"When I expected you to break through, I contacted the local Coven Head. I was already Queen of the Underworld at that point, so I didn't want to risk contacting Jess and having anyone draw a connection between us, but I thought that I could do something to help. To make sure that you were taken care of.

"But while she had been keeping tabs on you, she said that you showed no signs of breaking through. I told her to tell me if that changed, but she didn't reach out again."

"Not even when I did break through?"

"Well, no, but that was probably because she knew that you were heading to Ember Academy at that point. Some close friends of mine got tangled in a political mess in the Underworld, and they were exiled. I knew that their children would need somewhere safe to learn magic, just as you would. Esme proposed several projects between Witches and Demons, but I focused everything on the school. By the time you finally did break through, it was here waiting for you, and my friends' children still have a few years before they break through. Which gives us a few years to expand the student body beyond just Witches. Assuming that I can keep the Council of Light at bay for that long..."

"Do you really think they'll try to shut down the school?"

"I'm almost sure of it. But I'm also sure that a lot of Witches want the school to stay open. This won't be an easy fight for the Council.

"Though, it would be an easier fight for me if I understood every part of it. And what exactly you were doing befriending Maria Brown of all people."

"Didn't Mr Stiles tell you?"

Freya frowned. "Mr Stiles? Oh, right, Aaron." She smiled. "You know that that's not his real name, right? It's just an alias while working at the school. And you can call him Aaron. He is practically your brother-in-law."

"Yeah, but he's a teacher. It would be weird."

Freya sighed. "Yeah, I guess I can understand that. And as for what he told me, he said that Maria Brown tricked everyone into thinking she was Mary Maltere, a modern-day Witch. And then she convinced you to use a spell fuelled by his life force."

"I didn't know what was fuelling the spell," I said quickly. "And Maria... She woke up in a world that remembered her as a monster, and her coven was still frozen. She didn't think that she could ask for help and she panicked, not thinking that she could come up with another way to free them on her own. Not that anything excuses trying to kill someone, but..."

Freya, to my surprise, placed a hand on my arm to stop me, giving me an understanding look. "She made a mistake. And I'm the last person able to judge someone for that. I've made too many of my own."

I nodded, half-tempted to ask her what she meant by that, but then deciding against it, the slight ripple of her Energy beneath her skin telling me that the question wouldn't be welcomed.

"Aaron was unconscious," Freya continued, "so I've been hearing the rest third-hand."

I looked down at my hand in Nature's fur, knowing that Freya was prompting me to tell her the rest, but having to take a moment to sort out my words.

"I didn't know that she was drawing Mr Stiles' life-force. But Natalie, my roommate, figured it out, and she stopped me. Maria then fled the school, but... I started dreaming of her. Something about the spell along with previous times I'd interfered with her magic created a link between us. And when I slept, I kind of projected myself to her."

"And that's when she explained why she'd done the spell?"

I nodded. "I didn't trust her at first," I said, wanting Freya to know that I wasn't naïve. "It took a long time. But when the Amazons heard that I had been powerful enough to help Maria, they came to the school and demanded that I go through their trials, saying that they would only let me stay at the school if I passed them. Only they had no intention of letting me pass. But Maria helped me figure out how to get around their tampering with the trials."

"But it didn't work perfectly, did it?"

I sighed. "No. There was another girl taking the trials, and she found Willow countering the Amazons' tampering, so she turned her over." My jaw tightened as I glared at the ground. "Esme managed to uphold my passing marks, but they tried to take out their annoyance on Willow. She'd been a perfect student before then, so they couldn't get her expelled, but then when she defended me again by pulling down the wards so that you could save me from the Council..."

Freya grimaced. "The fact that she broke the rules to save you before meant that she could no longer hide behind a perfect record."

I nodded.

"I'm sorry, Amy. I know that it's not easy when your friends or family end up paying for the trouble you attract."

I almost asked her how she dealt with it, before stopping as I realised that I had my answer.

After all, that was why she'd left when I was little, wasn't it? The trouble she attracted had followed her back to me and our parents...

"Is it ever possible to keep your friends out of danger without leaving them?" I eventually asked. "Or will they be in danger as long as I'm here...?"

Freya sighed but then turned to me, her gaze firmly resolute. "It's never easy to protect them, Amy. I won't lie and say that it is. But part of figuring out how to protect them is realising that you can protect each other. That you're not in this alone, even if it feels like it. Even if the Council's target is currently on your back, you're not the only one they've ever hurt, and you're not the only one who can fight them.

"I'm going to guess that Willow wasn't just targeted because you care about her. I doubt the Council or the Amazons could have done what they did to her to a pure-blooded Witch."

I flinched. "But doesn't that make it worse? She was more vulnerable, and I dragged her into danger when she should have been keeping her head down."

"But that's my point, Amy. She was always in danger. You didn't drag her into anything. She could have chosen not to help you with the Amazon's trials, and she could have chosen not to lower the wards and call me to the school. She made the decision to stand up and fight alongside you. And the Council gave her plenty of reason to do it beyond hurting you.

"And tell me this, Amy; if your positions were reversed, would you have stood up to protect her? To fight alongside her?"

"Of course," I say, not hesitating for even a moment.

"Then remember that when you're feeling the need to blame yourself for all of this. Trust me, Amy, I've made the mistake of trying to protect someone to the point that you drive them away. People are capable of making the decision to stand beside you or not on their own. Let them."

I nodded, though while my rational mind understood her words, they weren't penetrating the fog of self-blame that had settled over me since the day before.

If I had just been smarter about dealing with the Council...

Freya sighed and I realised that my thoughts must be clear across my features.

But Freya didn't berate me for not listening to her. No, she just shook her head.

"You're too much like me, you know?" She eventually said. "And... If I had just been there for you before now... Amy, I am so sorry. I was sure that staying away would be better for you. That being tied to the Queen of the Underworld would only cause you problems. But now, I'm not so sure..."

I shrugged. "To be fair, Mr Stiles did offer to take me to the Underworld. I just... I think it would have caused as many problems as it solved. Especially because it might have made people more likely to realise that I was Angelborn, and that's the last thing that would have helped."

Freya sighed, pulling her lips into a grim line. "I guess you're right. But... I'm still sorry. I wish I could have been there for you. But I can be here now, at least."

"How long are you staying for?"

"As long as you need. And as long as it takes to make sure that the school is safe. I spent years making sure this school could start, I'm not going to let the Council tear it down now."

I frowned, focusing on the soft feel of Nature's fur between my fingers. "Do you really think they'll try?"

"I'm sure of it. But I've got people keeping an eye on them. Hopefully, we'll catch them before their plans get too far underway."

I stroked Nature a few more times, thinking over my next words before I spoke.

Making sure that I wanted to risk my idea.

But we needed all the help we could get.

"Councilwoman White's daughter works with the Guardians. Her name is Maureen. She doesn't really like her mother, and she needs your help. She's a Guide, but her partner was a Demon before the Council killed him. And she's pregnant. She's already lost one child, but if you were to help, like you did with me..."

Freya frowned. "You're suggesting that I create another Angelborn? Amy, I'm still not sure how I created you in the first place. All I remember is Margaret and Ryan constantly on edge and snapping at everything because their efforts to have a child weren't working. I just wanted to help, and I guess my wanting to help was enough. But there was a magical excess at the time and that may have helped with tapping into subconscious thoughts with my magic."

I sighed. "You know, if a married couple are snapping at each other, maybe a baby isn't the best solution."

"In my defence, they were fighting *because* they couldn't have a baby. Also, I was about your age, and I'd never had a family before them, so I wasn't exactly well-versed in such things. And even if they're fighting again now, I can't say that I regret making sure that you came into the world."

I managed a small smile at that.

"So," Freya said, "are they fighting?"

I rolled my eyes. "I think they have to be talking to fight. Dad got his memories of you back before I did. Apparently memory spells never really work on him. When Mum woke up and found out... Well, she wasn't happy that he kept your existence from her. Or the fact that I might grow up to be a Witch."

"Yeah... I can't say I'd be happy with that either. I mean, the only reason I was okay with the fact that Damon had been pretending to be Human and keeping magic from me when we got together was because I was doing the same thing. But as soon as things got serious... Well, I was ready to break it off before the truth came out. I couldn't live a lie like that.

"If we had already been married when I found out about magic... Well, I couldn't imagine keeping that from him. Especially if it involved our daughter."

"Yeah, I know. But that doesn't make the situation easier..."

"No, I imagine not." Freya sighed. "I wish that I had a solution. Some way to bridge the gap between Humans and magical beings. It's caused me no end of trouble over the years, and that's without romantic entanglements with Humans who don't already know about our world. We need some way to keep this kind of problem from happening, but I have to admit, for all my power, both magical and political, I'm at a loss."

"Maureen said the Guardians were working on a few ideas. Like trying to make their home city a safe haven where Humans could know about magic when they were there and forget when they left, or trying to recreate the Twilight's spell so that Humans and magical beings can't hurt each other."

"Yeah, Alex – my heartbond – hinted that they might be working on something like that. Something that might need the kind of power only an Angel can provide." She sighed. "I wish that I could help them, I really do, but... Some of the founders of the Guardians were exiled from the Underworld for treason. I can't be seen helping them in any way."

"Not even a little? I mean, surely if it helps everyone..."

Freya shook her head. "No. I am bound by Fate, unfortunately."

"Yeah, Esme mentioned something about prophecies. But are they really so dire?"

Freya took a moment before saying, "If I tell you, I have to swear you to secrecy."

"Okay, fine."

I felt the magic wash over me as Freya cast the spell non-verbally before continuing.

"My daughter, Katherine, doesn't have magic."

"Oh..." I said, as it took me a moment to realise what that meant. "But she's the Princess of the Underworld."

"I know. And my instinct would be to give up the crown immediately, move us all back to Earth and raise her there, where I could help the Guardians without issue. But... Well, an Oracle I trust made it clear that my best course of action is to actually keep the throne and wait until... Well, I'm not sure what. Something."

"Both Charlotte and Esme told me not to chase prophecies. Charlotte had one that seems to be about me, but I've just been ignoring it."

Freya frowned. "Well, you can try, but if it warns of trouble..."

I shrugged. "It wasn't that clear. Apparently Charlotte can only see the future when she's almost black-out drunk, so the prophecies are always a bit messy. Something about 'healing the rift', but that could mean anything."

"Yes, unfortunately it could. But if it was important enough to draw her sight... Well, I'm not suggesting that your friend get black-out drunk again, but it probably wouldn't hurt if she tried to learn how to control her powers. I'm all for fighting Fate if you want, but you do have to understand what you're fighting."

I nodded, not sure that I had the brain space to think on that right now.

No, everything felt foggy and slow.

Or, well, foggier than I could expect on a bad day before I took my medication.

Freya gave me an understanding smile. "You don't need to think about any of this right now, though. Come on, why don't you tell me about the other things I missed?"

I STAYED WITH FREYA for most of the day, not ready to head back.

She assured me that I wouldn't be expected back in lessons, so I spent the day getting to know her again instead.

It was strange how easily I managed to slip back into our familiar relationship, but I was just thankful for it.

Freya never once reacted to Maria's name with obvious disdain, and I needed that.

I needed someone who understood why I was upset, not someone who was happy to let her die.

Still, as the winter sun began to fade and the school day ended, I knew that it was time to head back.

"Okay," Freya said when I suggested it, and I was thankful for the simple understanding.

We headed back through to the woods outside the school, Nature's clearing leaving us in the same place we'd entered it.

"I'm just going to be staying in the guest rooms in the administration building if you need me," Freya said.

I nodded. "Okay. I'll see you later."

Freya smiled. "See you."

I headed towards classes, intending to catch Willow as she left.

But then I stopped dead in my tracks.

Willow wouldn't be leaving classes today.

No, she'd left the school.

She was gone.

Dark Energy crackled under my skin at the memory as my throat tightened.

I kept going towards the classrooms.

I needed to work off this Dark Energy. All of this festering fury and helplessness threatening to spill forth.

If I didn't...

I pushed away memories of when I first came into my magic.

I wasn't going to hurt anyone now. I had more control now than then, after all.

That control had just never been tested like this before...

Luckily, I found Mr Stiles just as he was leaving his classroom.

"Amelia. Are you okay? After what happened yesterday, I mean-"

"I'm fine," I snapped, in a way that I was sure contradicted my words. "I just... Are we doing combat training tonight?"

He hesitated for just a moment, looking me over before nodding with a sigh. "Yeah, just shift to the gym and I'll meet you there in a moment."

I nodded, shifting there immediately.

A moment later, Mr Stiles arrived, along with another Demon.

Prince Damon.

"Amelia," Mr Stiles said with a smile, "this is Damon, my heartbond. And your brother-in-law, I suppose."

I suddenly became hyper aware of the fact that I was still in my clothes from the day before, mud stains all over my clothes and skin.

Still, Damon gave me a good-natured smile. "Amelia, it's good to finally meet you."

I nodded. "Likewise."

Damon cringed. "You're just brimming with Dark Energy right now, aren't you? It's unusual to see this much from a Witch, rather than a powerful Demon. Which probably makes it a good thing I'm here."

He turned to Mr Stiles with a smirk. "She might have actually killed you."

Mr Stiles rolled his eyes. "Har-har." His expression then softened as he looked me over. "Though, yes, you might want to take over her training today. Assuming that's okay with you, Amelia? Damon is a better teacher than me."

I nodded, a little curious to see just how much better Prince Damon was than Mr Stiles, though mostly, I just needed to get rid of this excess Energy before I lost control of it.

Prince Damon approached, looking me over once more. "What weapons have you trained with?"

"Weapons?"

"So, just your wand, then?"

I nodded. "I didn't even know that I was allowed weapons on school grounds."

Prince Damon turned to Mr Stiles with a raised eyebrow.

Mr Stiles shrugged. "There are Magical Self-Defence classes, but yes, they focus on wands, mostly. Though, if you wanted to train Amelia with a sword, I'm sure Gail wouldn't mind."

Prince Damon nodded as he turned back to me. "Perhaps you should just attack me and we'll go from there."

"Okay," I said, just barely managing to get the word out before I channeled my Energy into my muscles, speeding and strengthening them before I ran at Prince Damon, striking with everything I had.

He clearly wasn't expecting such a sudden attack and my blast hit him straight in his chest, knocking him back several paces.

He smiled before turning to Mr Stiles. "Yeah, she definitely would have hurt you with that one."

I went to strike again, but he moved far faster than I could even see, catching my fist in his hand.

"Argh!" I kicked him in the side, trying to pull myself free.

It probably wouldn't have worked, but another blast of Dark Energy coursed through me, knocking me free.

I panted for breath as exhaustion set in.

Well, I'd needed to work off my Dark Energy, but those two blasts had taken everything I'd had.

Prince Damon didn't try to take advantage of my exhaustion.

Instead, he looked me over while I continued to struggle for breath.

He gestured to his armour. "So, I'm wearing the strongest armour ever made in the Underworld. Most people wouldn't be able to do anything to me right now, but you still knocked me back. Twice."

I looked away, Dark Energy riling once more as I couldn't shake one simple thought.

If I was so powerful, why couldn't I save Maria?

Damon eyed me warily as he saw my Energy start to crackle.

"Okay, I think those two hits were enough of a work out for anyone for one night." He stepped closer with a reassuring look. "Aaron has done a good job in training you. But not everything can be solved with fighting, Amelia. What the Council did... You can't fight away how you feel about that."

I glared at him. "I don't need your pity."

"That's not what this is. It's concern. You're powerful, but you're pouring your pain into your magic, rather than dealing with it, and it's exhausting you."

I continued to glare, but I couldn't help but become acutely aware of how my hands were shaking as magical exhaustion set it.

I might be Angelborn, and I might be powerful, but I still had limits.

That cut deeper, somehow.

At least if I had been capable of saving Maria, then I could blame myself. I could turn all this anger inward and have a target I could really hurt.

But accepting that even as powerful as I was, I had limits... That Maria had been right to tell me not to fight...

Well, then the only targets for my anger were the very people I hadn't been able to fight.

So how could I fight them now?

"You should get some rest," Prince Damon said. "You've had a long couple of days, and exhausting your magic like this won't have helped."

I nodded, knowing that he was right and not really having the strength to argue.

"And Amelia?" he said before I left. "Don't forget, you're not alone. Freya and I are here for you."

I just nodded again, not sure what I could say to that.

Sure, they were *physically* here, but Freya was bound by Fate and politics.

Fate and politics that had stopped her from being there for me before Maria was killed.

I shifted out of the gym and to my bedroom, not sure I could handle continuing the conversation further.

"Amy!" Natalie said as I appeared. "Are you all right? Where have you been all day?"

"I was with Freya," I managed to mutter. "And I think I just need a shower and sleep."

Thankfully, Natalie nodded. "Okay. Well, I'll just be here if you need me."

I forced a small smile. "Thanks."

I STRUGGLED AGAINST the chains holding me, the metal wrapped tightly around my body as I fought to get free.

I had to do it. I had to save her.

But then a sword flashed as it arced into the sky.

And was brought down on Maria's head.

"No!"

I awoke with a gasp, a thin coat of sweat covering me.

"Amy?" Natalie asked, her voice groggy as she pushed herself up from her bed. "Are you okay?"

"Yeah," I managed, cursing the shake in my voice. "Just a bad dream. I'm okay, you should go back to sleep."

Natalie ignored my words, instead grabbing her blanket and moving faster than I could see.

Until she was suddenly next to me, wrapping my own blanket around me.

"I really am fine."

"Okay," she said.

She didn't move away.

And I didn't have the strength to protest further.

Not when having her beside me helped calm my shaking hands.

"Think you can go back to sleep?" she asked.

"Not for a while," I admitted.

"Well, I was going to look for new Civ mods anyway. Want to help?"

"Yeah," I said as she grabbed her laptop and I shifted over to give her more room on the small bed. "Sounds fun."

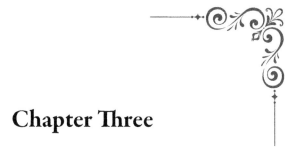

Chapter Three

I awoke slowly, not chased from my sleep by nightmares.

And also not having gone to Maria's tower.

I did my best to suppress tears at that, the effort helped by curling up to the luke-warm body next to me.

At least, until I remembered that I had fallen asleep next to Natalie.

After she'd seen me waking up from a nightmare.

Creator, she must have thought I was pathetic.

And then she'd fallen asleep next to me, despite the fact that the last time she'd done that, she'd woken up in a panic about how close we were getting.

Natalie stirred next to me and I braced myself, expecting her to pull away as soon as she realised what had happened.

But she didn't.

Instead she gave me a small smile as she awoke. "Hey. How are you?"

"All right. Are you okay? I mean, last time we woke up like this..."

"Last time we woke up like this, I was worried about losing control and biting you."

"And you're not now?"

She shrugged. "No. Last time, I nearly bit you because we were kissing. Because we were just pretending that we didn't have feelings for each other. But now you're in love with Willow, so I don't think there's any danger of us kissing again. To be honest, it's kind of a relief. To at least be this close with someone without worrying about potentially biting them."

I smiled, doing my best to ignore the strange way my stomach twisted at Natalie's absolute certainty that kissing was off the table.

It had no reason to twist. She was right. I was in love with Willow.

And I would have her back as soon as I could, and we would bond, and everything would be fine.

And for now, Natalie had kept the nightmares at bay and the last thing I wanted was to complicate that.

So, I refused to think more on it.

"I should probably get ready for classes," Natalie said as she checked the time on her phone. "Are you coming, or are you spending the day with Freya again?"

"Going to classes, I think. I need to actually do something and distract myself, rather than just spending all day crying again."

"Okay. But you know that it's okay if you need to-"

"I know," I said, cutting her off. "I just... Whether or not I need it, I don't think I can handle it. No, I need to just keep moving."

Thankfully, Natalie nodded and I headed to the bathroom to get dressed.

WE HEADED DOWN TO BREAKFAST as soon as we were dressed, and I picked up a pastry and coffee before walking over to the table where Lena and Charlotte were sitting.

I bit my lip as Natalie and I sat down, making the empty chair next to me painfully obvious.

"Lia," Lena said, drawing my attention from the empty chair with a tone that was surprisingly soft coming from her, "how are you holding up? You know, after everything."

I looked down at my coffee, wishing that everyone would just stop talking about it. "I'm fine."

Thankfully, Lena didn't press me further.

I glanced back to Willow's empty chair before pulling out my phone.

She hadn't texted or called or anything...

I turned to Lena. "Have you heard from Willow since she left?"

Lena shook her head. "I texted her, but I got a stock reply, saying that she's unavailable. Some really paranoid covens have protections to stop a phone signal getting in or out, and they send similar responses, but I don't remember Willow saying that her coven ever had them."

I immediately went to type a message, my stomach twisting with guilt at having not done so before.

Hey

I left it at that, not sure what else to say.

I was so annoyed at people asking me how I was, I didn't want to do the same here.

I got a response almost instantly.

The person you are trying to contact is unavailable right now. Please try again later.

I sighed, running my hand through my hair. If I wasn't allowed to text her, maybe I wouldn't be allowed to talk to her at all.

Charlotte tucked a loose strand of hair behind her ear. "Do you think she went to a new coven? Why wouldn't she just go home?"

"I don't think she went to a new coven," I admitted as I picked at my pastry. "I think she went to join her father."

Lena frowned. "You mean her father the assassin? But you just mean she's visiting him, right? Not that she's... Like, following in his footsteps or anything."

I shrugged.

Lena shook her head. "No, that's ridiculous. Willow would never."

I just shrugged again, far from sure of that.

"Look," I eventually said, "after everything with the Amazons... Willow started carrying around the blade her father gave her. And she was talking about understanding the *Fin'Hathan* mission a bit more. Their mission to stop corruption. And then the Council got her expelled in an obvious example of corruption..."

Lena looked far from happy, but she also didn't argue with me.

She just muttered, "Shit," under her breath before stabbing at her cereal with her spoon.

"You can't say that she doesn't have a point," I said. "I mean, we can't just let the Council get away with this shit. We can't just sit back and do nothing."

"We haven't been doing nothing. If you'll remember, Charlotte and I helped with Esme's election campaign. And she won."

"And then the Council ignored her, choosing to listen to Dana instead, even though the Amazons didn't elect her. The Council don't care about the rules, they just do what they want."

"Yeah, they do that because they can. They have the backing of the Slayers, the Guides, and the Light covens. Not all of them agree with them, but it's either follow their rules or go it alone. Hell, if Maria Brown couldn't stand up to them, who the hell could?"

"Maria couldn't stand up to them because she was alone," I said, remembering what Maureen had told me about standing together. "She didn't even try to work with others, but I think she would have had allies if she had. The Council have pissed off a lot of people over the years."

"They might have, but even if you're right, they would have to be pissed off enough to do something about it, and the fact that no one has yet tells me that they're not."

Charlotte frowned. "People cared enough to back Esme in the last Amazon election. They didn't win by just sitting around, Witches like Esme were working in the background for years before the opportunity came up to make real change. And the Guardians got enough people to care to build a community independent of the Council."

"That's not the same thing as a revolution, Lottie."

The bell rang before we could continue arguing, and Lena hurriedly stood up and grabbed her bag, clearly done with the conversation.

"I'll see you at break," she said before heading off.

I sighed, looking down at my mostly uneaten breakfast before grabbing my coffee and getting up myself.

I COMPLETELY ZONED out of my morning classes.

It wasn't on purpose – I was trying – but what was normally difficult for me was now impossible.

It was so hard to care about my Human studies now. Who cared what I got on my A-Levels? Was I seriously just going to head to university as if I could just slot back into my old life?

Lena and the others pointedly didn't bring up either Willow or Maria again over either break or lunch, and I decided to just let it go, not wanting to start another fight.

In all honesty, I wasn't sure that Lena was wrong. Maybe no one would help me fight the Council.

But the one thing I was sure of was the fact that it wouldn't stop me.

By the time I arrived at my double Potions lesson that afternoon, I was bored to the point of painful frustration, incapable of keeping my thoughts from my fury at the Council.

Fury that had my Dark Energy crackling just beneath my skin, which certainly didn't help my concentration.

Still, I managed to keep it under control, and if anyone else noticed, they didn't say.

Auntie Jess entered the class as I reached my desk, and seeing her back teaching the class at least calmed me a little.

After everything that happened with the Council, it was easy to forget that I'd freed her from the binding spell. It seemed like such a small victory in the face of the loss that had followed... But still, I knew that I shouldn't be so quick to dismiss it.

The binding spell in question seemed to hum within me at the thought, the sudden wave of Maria's magic causing my eyes to sting with tears.

I blinked them away, clearing my throat.

I couldn't just burst into tears in class like a four-year-old.

No, I thought, taking a deep breath. I could do this. I could get through one normal school day...

"Good afternoon, girls," Auntie Jess said as she made her way behind her desk. "As you can see, I'm awake and teaching again. Mr Stiles told me that he let you choose your own projects, so most of you will still be working on those. If you need any help, feel free to come and ask me, and if you've finished with your project, I would like a short essay on what you felt you learned from the project."

All of the girls who'd been happy to have shorter projects now groaned, and I couldn't blame them.

Potions was a nice break from other lessons because of how practical it was. Sure, there was theory to understand, but Auntie Jess was a big believer in learning by doing.

As much as making the same potions over and over again to better understand them wasn't the most interesting experience, it was still a nice mental break from lectures and essays.

A break those girls now wouldn't get.

I headed to the cold storage cupboards to find my cauldron, still full of my resting potion.

I took out my wand, casting a spell to gently move my cauldron back over to my desk without spilling a drop.

Once it was settled, I pulled out my notes to remind myself of where I was, just as my auntie came over to my table.

"Don't other students need help?" I asked before she could speak, cursing myself as I realised how rude that probably seemed.

But I *knew* that she was going to try to ask me how I was and I just couldn't deal with that.

"No," she said, smiling despite my accidentally sharp tone. "It surprisingly seems that everyone is pretty happy with their projects for now. I just wanted to see how you were doing with yours. Everything going okay?"

"Yeah, fine. Now that it's rested, I should be able to finish it this afternoon."

She nodded. "Good, good. But if you need to head out early, just let me know. I wasn't expecting you to show up today, to be honest. I thought you might have wanted to spend some more time with Freya."

I shrugged. "I can see her after school."

"True. But... Well, after everything with the Council, I figured you might need a few days to yourself. Or to just recuperate and talk to someone. You know, if the problem is that things are awkward with Freya-"

"They're not," I assured her. "They're actually surprisingly not." I sighed. "I guess having part of her magic just makes her more familiar, despite not having seen her in years. Like when I went to talk to Nature."

"Well, that's good. But if you do need someone else to talk about this with-"

"I know," I said. "I really do. I just... If I keep myself busy, I can just pretend that it's fine. That she's not really gone, and Willow wasn't really forced to leave. And I would rather do that than... Than talk."

Auntie Jess frowned. "'She'? Oh, right, you mean Maria. That's what you're upset about?"

I looked up from my work to give her an incredulous look. "Of course it is! What else would it be?"

"The fact that the Council held you prisoner for days, where they tortured you, and I'd bet good money that they also weren't feeding you properly. And then even after they executed Maria, they still almost executed you. If Freya hadn't come when she did..."

"But she did, and I'm fine. Maria wasn't so lucky."

Auntie Jess sighed. "I know, Amy. And I don't know why she matters to you, but she had lived for centuries past her time. And she didn't belong here. Obviously, the Council killing anyone is bad, but-"

"Don't," I said, not caring how sharp my tone was this time. "Don't try to justify it. There's no excuse for the Council killing her. Like Freya said, Maria's only crime was hurting Mr Stiles, and it wasn't the Council's job to decide how she should be punished for that."

"Her only crime in this time. In the past-"

"You're talking about centuries ago, and are you really so sure that records going back that far are accurate? The Council literally admitted to me that they knew that she wasn't the monster history made her out to be, but they were worried that she would threaten their authority. Just like they worried that properly prosecuting the Slayers who killed your husband would."

Auntie Jess flinched and my anger drained as I realised that I might have gone too far by bringing up my late uncle.

Still, Auntie Jess sighed. "Okay, I get it. The Council aren't trustworthy. And while I don't think there's an excuse for hurting Aaron... I actually liked Maria. Back when she was 'Mary'. After Aaron was hurt, I assumed that had always been an act, and I still can't reconcile the two, but... Maybe there was more truth to it than I thought."

"Her coven is still frozen," I said. "That's why she hurt Mr Stiles. She blamed herself and wanted to set them free. And the quickest way to do that was with a sacrifice. I'm not saying she should have hurt him, but even she admitted that she was wrong. And she helped me to finally lift the spell once and for all."

Auntie Jess nodded. "Okay," was all she said, but that was enough for me as I refocused on my work, really not wanting to talk about this anymore.

Auntie Jess stayed silent for several moments, watching me work, and I wished that there was a polite way to ask her to leave.

Eventually, she said, "Amy, have you thought about maybe taking a break from all of this?"

"All of this?"

"The magical world. I know that it's nice to be at the school, where you don't have to hide your magic, but after everything you've been through... Maybe going home for a bit wouldn't be the worst idea. Christmas isn't that far off. I'm sure no one would mind if you went home early and came back in January. And your mum was asking after you. I'm sure she would be glad to have you back for a while."

"I'll think about it," I said, not wanting to start an argument.

But I knew without a doubt that the last thing I needed was to go home and spend time in the middle of my parents' crumbling marriage.

Thankfully, at that, my auntie nodded. "Well, I should do the rounds and make sure no one else needs any help."

As soon as she left my desk, I grabbed my headphones from my bag and stuck them on, thanking my auntie's lax policy on wearing them during practicals.

Hopefully, with them on, she would get the message and not try to talk to me again.

I MANAGED TO GET THROUGH my lesson without having to talk to anyone else, and as soon as I heard the bell through my headphones, I hurried out of the room, though I left them on.

I rushed out into the corridor, only to run headlong into Freya.

The rest of the students gave her a wide berth in the corridor, and I couldn't blame them. Even in her plain black clothes, she was still tall and obviously muscular, making her an intimidating figure before you took into account the aura of power that seemed to radiate from her.

My magic recognised hers as kin, but I imagined everyone else's was perking to attention at the presence of someone so obviously powerful.

"Amy," she greeted as I pulled off my headphones, "would you mind if we had a word?"

"Of course not," I said before following as she turned and headed outside.

Once we were out of earshot of the other students, heading towards the edge of the woods, she said, "I was wondering how you're feeling. Are you doing okay today?"

I shrugged. "I guess. I've just been trying to keep myself distracted."

"And school does that for you? I was always bored senseless..."

"Well, that has been my problem today, yes."

Freya smiled. "I imagine you want to retain some normalcy, but maybe I can talk to Gail about setting up some advanced classes while I'm here. For now, are you okay to discuss Maria?"

I tensed instinctively, but forced myself to nod. "I guess. What did you want to talk about?"

"You were the closest thing she had to family. That means that you're the most appropriate person to decide... Well, to decide how to say goodbye."

I frowned. "You mean like a funeral? Is there even a point when no one else would come?"

"Even if you're correct that no one else would want to say goodbye to her, you should still see her off properly, Amy. For your own sense of closure, if nothing else."

I bit my lip, my gaze dropping to the soft grass as we continued to head towards the woods at a slow pace, the presence of nature the only thing giving me resolve. "I guess you're right. But... I don't really know how to organise something like that."

"I'll take care of the details, if you want. I just need to know what kind of ritual you want to use. Nature tells me that Witches of Maria's age used to return their dead to her. We could do that, if you think that's what Maria would have wanted."

I nodded, Maria's knowledge giving me details of the ritual Freya was talking about. "Yeah, I think she would have liked that."

"Then, if you think you'll be ready, I can set everything up for tomorrow night."

"Yeah, okay," I said, not sure how delaying it would help.

Freya's phone buzzed in her pocket and she pulled it out before reading the message with a smile. "Damon has just returned from the Underworld with Kath." She turned to me. "Would you like to come and meet your niece?"

I nodded, more than a little caught off guard by that. I knew that Freya had a daughter, but I never really equated that with me being an aunt.

Freya headed back towards the administration building and I followed alongside.

I tensed as we entered, and it took me a moment to realise that I was expecting to still see Slayer guards there.

But no, they'd left with the Council.

After all, there wasn't a prisoner to guard here anymore.

"You okay?" Freya asked, and I cursed my obvious reaction.

"Yeah, just... The Council used this building to hold Maria before they..."

"Ah," Freya said. "I can ask Damon to meet us somewhere else."

"No, it's okay. I'm okay. I promise."

Freya regarded me for a moment before nodding, and I let out a breath of relief.

Being here wasn't easy, but the only thing worse I could imagine was everyone making a fuss.

We headed downstairs to the corridor where Maria's cell had been.

Thankfully, Freya moved to a door across the hall, confirming my suspicion that the cell had, in fact, been a repurposed guest room.

Sitting on the edge of the large bed in the centre of the room was Prince Damon, but much like Freya, he was in a simple black t-shirt and jeans, rather than his more formal garb.

Standing next to him was a young girl, who looked somewhere between seven and ten, but given how tall her parents were, I wasn't willing to take a more accurate guess.

Especially not when she was the spitting image of Freya, with her inky black hair, pale skin, and wild green eyes.

She was smiling when we entered, but it faded as she saw me, and she stepped behind her father, her hands going to fidget with the skirts of her black and crimson velvet dress.

"Kath," Freya said, "this is my younger sister. Your Auntie Amy."

The girl looked me over cautiously. "You're not a Demon," she eventually said.

"No, I'm not," I said. "I'm a Witch."

Freya moved over to her daughter. "Just like your Auntie Alice is an Oracle. And your sister is Human. Not all family is the same, Kath."

Kath nodded, seeming a little less wary as she turned back to me.

I frowned as Freya stood up. "You have another daughter?"

"No," Freya said, with a smile and a shake of her head, "my heartbond has a daughter with her wife. Damon and I don't spend enough time with Cassy to really be considered her step-parents, but she and Kath have been inseparable for years."

Kath went to stand behind her mother, still slightly hiding from me, but speaking up without prompt. "Cassy doesn't come to the Underworld much, but I'm allowed to go to the secret hideout on Earth."

I raised an eyebrow. "Secret hideout?"

Freya answered before Kath could. "My heartbond's family situation is complicated. But it means that she's got possibly the most protected home on Earth. Which makes it safe enough for the Princess to visit without me or her father looking after her."

"And Alice? Is she just a family friend, or do you have another sister?"

"A bit of both, I suppose. I guess you might not remember, but Alice and I grew up together in the foster system before I went to live with your parents. She was the closest thing I had to family before that point.

"And speaking of Alice, she sent me some information on training young Seers. So, if your friend wants to see if she can expand her prophecy, I could help her."

I bit my lip. On the one hand, I didn't want to get sucked into trying to decipher the future. But given everything I was going up against if I was determined to make the Council answer for Maria's death... Well, maybe having an idea of what was coming might help.

"I'll ask her about it."

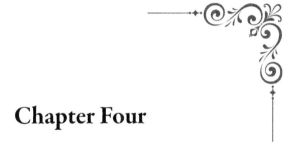

Chapter Four

I groaned as I awoke the next morning, shifting closer to the figure my arm was wrapped around, keeping her warmer than the morning before.

But then I pulled away, remembering that Natalie had sat next to me on my bed the night before while we'd passed my laptop back and forth, taking turns in Civ.

Then she'd suggested going to sleep, and I'd hesitated.

Natalie hadn't taken more than a moment to realise why, before suggesting that she stay with me, rather than moving back to her bed, in the hopes that it would keep the nightmares away.

I'd been too tired to object.

And she'd been right, I realised as I sat up, I hadn't had any nightmares.

But the fact that she was happy to sleep beside me for practical purposes didn't mean that she'd be happy with me snuggling up to her.

I pinched the bridge of my nose and sighed, trying to push back tears as I thought about how much simpler things would be if Willow was with me.

I could just sleep beside her, and wake up with my love in my arms, not worrying if I was crossing some kind of line with my friend.

Natalie stirred, moving to place a hand on my arm.

Where Dark Energy was crackling.

It mustn't have been enough to hurt her, though, as she didn't pull away.

"Amy..." she said, her voice echoing my own sorrow as I remembered that Energy was raw emotion. Touching mine must have shown her everything I was feeling... "You really miss Willow, don't you?"

I nodded, glad that that was all Natalie had felt from me as I turned to her. "I know that she's probably safe – that she's probably with her father, and that he'll look out for her – but I just wish that we could talk. She said that she was happy for me to stay here without her, and I know that she was probably right to say that I should, given that Freya's here, but... Well, I just wish that we were together, wherever we had to be to do that."

Natalie gently squeezed my arm. "Why don't you try messaging her again? Maybe she's not staying under protections."

"Yeah, maybe." I grabbed my phone from the bedside table and sent another quick "*Hey.*"

The same response as before appeared, just a moment later.

I sighed.

"Same response?" Natalie asked.

"Yuuup. I'm gonna head into the shower. You good to go down to breakfast once I'm done, or do you need it too?"

"I need it too, but I promise to be quick." She smiled. "I do have Vampire speed, after all."

WE HEADED DOWN TO BREAKFAST as soon as we were both showered and dressed, arriving to find Charlotte and Lena already there.

"Hey," I said as I sat down with my food and coffee.

"Hey," Lena said, only for Charlotte to nudge her almost immediately.

Lena turned to give her girlfriend a firm look. "I need to do small talk first. It's polite."

Charlotte turned bright red at that, looking away. "Sorry. I forgot."

I shrugged. "Well, if you want to cut to whatever you want to cut to, I'm sure I won't be offended. I also hate small talk. It's painfully boring."

Lena sighed. "Well, I at least wanted to give you a chance to eat something before I said something that might upset you."

I frowned. "Upset me?"

"Well, not *upset* you upset you, just that it might not be something you want to start your morning with. But I guess you probably heard the announcement this morning anyway, so maybe I'm just being foolish."

My frown deepened. "Announcement?"

Natalie turned to me. "You were in the shower, and I figured that you already knew, but Ms Griffin announced that Maria Brown's funeral would be tonight."

"Oh," I said, looking down at my coffee. "Well, I don't know why she would bother. I mean, it's not like anyone but me is going to go."

"We're going," Lena said firmly. "That's what Charlotte wanted me to say. We're both going. We're your friends and she was your mentor. Of course we're going to stand by you through this."

I took a moment to process that. With how distrustful everyone had been of Maria... Well, as much as my friends had helped me try to help Maria escape, that didn't mean that they wanted to attend her funeral.

"Thanks," I eventually said. "That means a lot."

Lena gave me an understanding smile as I picked up my coffee and sipped it, despite it still being a little too hot to drink.

I wanted to try to wash away the tears forming behind my eyes before they had a chance to fall.

Creator, I couldn't keep doing this. I had to pull myself together.

I finally felt able to put the mug down after downing half the contents, though I could no longer feel my tongue.

I picked up my pastry and sighed. It probably would have been a better idea to eat it before I burned my mouth.

Back when I could enjoy it...

A shadow fell over the table and I frowned as I turned to see who was approaching.

My frown only deepened as I realised that it was Victoria.

Victoria who hadn't said two words to me since my first morning at the school, when I'd made the mistake of trying to talk to her.

And she'd made it perfectly clear what she'd thought of the fact that both of my parents were Human.

I braced myself, sure that her opinion hadn't changed. And had probably only gotten worse since Nature had awoken the part of her magic that resided inside of me, my right eye now a wild green, signalling to everyone that I wasn't just a Witch.

"Amelia," she said, her voice and expression as haughty as ever, "Ms Griffin's announcement said that Maria Brown's funeral would be tonight-"

"*Don't*," I growl, standing up as Dark Energy crackled under my skin, my chair scraping hard on the wooden floor.

I knew exactly where she was going.

She was trying to dig her claws into a fresh wound so that she could rip it open and fill it with salt.

And why? Because I was an easy target? Because she didn't think I belonged at the school?

"Don't you dare start with me today," I continued, my voice growing louder with each word. "The Council of Light killed Maria in cold blood just because they thought she *might* threaten their authoritarian rule. And she let them because she was worried about what they would do to me if they didn't. If you think I have any patience for petty bullshit right now, you are sorely mistaken."

Victoria just stared at me with wide eyes and I suddenly realised how silent the room was.

And that everyone was looking at me.

My throat tightened and I struggled to draw in breath.

Creator, I was used to everyone thinking I was crazy due to impulsive outbursts, but I thought I'd managed to avoid that reputation here.

But now?

Before I could finally take in shallow, panicked breaths, however, Victoria dropped her gaze.

"I'm sorry," she said, the words shocking me more than any others could.

Victoria was sorry?

Why? She didn't have to say that. She could have laughed at me and everyone here would have laughed along.

Look at the crazy girl who actually dared to *care* about something, isn't it funny how broken she is?

"You're right," Victoria continued, "this wasn't a good time."

And at that, she left.

I sat back down as the sound of the room returned to the low hum of chattering voices.

I turned to the others, who looked just as confused as I was.

"What the hell do you think that was about?" Lena asked.

Charlotte raised an eyebrow. "Do you mean the fact that Victoria came over here, or the fact that she apologised and left?"

Lena shrugged. "Either." She turned to me. "Do you really think she meant to start shit?"

"It's Victoria. What else could she have wanted?"

"Good point..."

At that, the bell rang, and I couldn't help but be a little relieved as I picked up my coffee and headed to class.

CLASSES CONTINUED TO bore me.

And it wasn't just the Human classes. As I sat in Basics of Spellcraft after lunch, I found that every word the teacher spoke was overly familiar.

And of course it was.

There might be a new teacher, but Maria had written the course.

And I had her knowledge now.

I knew everything the new teacher was trying to tell me, inside and out.

History of Magic wasn't much better.

"You okay?" Mr Stiles asked, making his way over to me as everyone else wrote their essays.

And I doodled in my notebook.

"I'm finished," I said.

He raised an eyebrow. "Finished? You wrote two pages? In normal-sized handwriting?"

I passed him three pages of A4.

"Part of the bond between me and Maria gave me access to her knowledge, and you asked us to write essays about the Demon monarchy."

"*The State of Demonic Politics Following the Death of Queen Maltess*," Mr Stiles read aloud.

I shrugged. "Maria had a lot of strong opinions on the matter."

"I can imagine," he said. "You know, you could have mentioned this before the essay. Maria was frozen for more recent history."

"I know. Sorry. Just once I thought of this topic... Well, I guess I just went into hyperfocus a bit."

He gave me an understanding smile. "It's okay. I think that's more than understandable today. And I've actually got to admit that I'm looking forward to reading your essay."

I nodded, though I'd stopped really listening to anything he'd said after he'd said that my hyperfocus was understandable *today*.

And I had remembered that this was my last lesson.

And what exactly tonight was.

The bell rang, signalling that my time ignoring what was coming was well and truly up.

I slowly picked up my things and headed out of the room, the last one out of the door.

Well, except for Natalie, who packed up faster than me, but still stood waiting for me.

"Hey," she said as we headed out into the corridor, "want to pick up some early dinner?"

I nodded, despite the fact that I wasn't sure I'd be able to keep anything down.

But I didn't have the strength to actually say that, so I just followed Natalie to the dining hall and picked up a sandwich, given that it was the only thing I could really face.

I still only picked at it as we sat at the dining table.

Lena and Charlotte joined us, and they talked with Natalie, but I didn't have the wherewithal to contribute.

I just sat, picking at my food and trying to focus on their chatter rather than my anxiety.

But focusing at will had never been my strong point.

Eventually, Natalie turned to me. "We should probably head to our room and get changed."

I looked down at my uniform, realising that it probably wasn't suitable for a funeral.

But I didn't have much else.

I still had the black dress I'd worn to my grandfather's funeral, but was that appropriate for this kind of ceremony?

Maria's knowledge told me no, but I didn't have the appropriate robes, and I didn't expect that my friends did either.

But I just nodded and followed Natalie as she left the dining room, my sandwich remaining largely untouched.

We headed up to our room, and as soon as we entered, I opened the wardrobe and just stared at the options.

"Not sure what to wear?" Natalie asked after a while.

I turned to see that she was in a black tunic dress with red accents that brought out her eyes, though the design seemed more functional than decorative, with dark leather leggings beneath it.

"What's that?" I asked, nodding to the crimson design at her breast. Almost like a series of roses twisted around each other, thorns and petals equally prominent in the design.

Natalie glanced down at the design on her dress. "Oh, that's just the sigil of my Nest. My grandmother basically acts as the matriarch. My Vampire grandmother, that is. She gave me this when she heard I was going to Ember. It's kind of a traditional battle dress for Witches. It's got healing spells woven into it."

I nodded, Maria's knowledge telling me that a battle dress would be appropriate.

Except I didn't have one...

I turned as someone knocked at the door.

"Come in," I said with a frown, wondering who it could be.

The door opened and Freya walked through.

"Hi, Amy."

She turned to Natalie. "I don't believe we've met before. I'm-"

"Queen Freya," Natalie finished for her before bowing. "I know. I'm Natalie. Amy's roommate."

Freya shifted awkwardly at the move before turning to me. "So... Does she know...?"

"That you're my sister and I'm Angelborn? Yes. Natalie's my best friend, and she's been drawn into most of the drama around here."

Freya nodded turning back to Natalie. "Well then I really must insist that you don't use my title. Or bow. Just 'Freya' is okay. If my sister trusts you then so do I."

Natalie blushed slightly and nodded. "Thank you Qu- *Freya*."

Freya smiled, though it was bittersweet. "You know, I almost miss the days when no one knew who I was."

I raised an eyebrow. "Almost?"

She shrugged. "Well, back before anyone knew I was an Angel, they figured I was just a mongrel. Such a mix of magical and Human blood that no one community would ever accept me. That was less than fun, and I can't say that I miss the feeling of being without a community. But still, I wasn't alone in not having a community, and maybe if we'd banded together like Caroline and Persephone have done with the Guardians..."

She shook her head. "Well, anyway, I didn't come here to talk about the past. I came because it occurred to me that you might not have anything to wear tonight."

"I- No, actually, I don't."

"For someone who has seen battle, it's appropriate to wear your armour." She nodded to Natalie as an example. "And while what the Council have put you through would certainly count as a battle, I thought you might not have armour."

"No, I don't. It's not really come up."

"Well then." Freya waved her hand, shifting in a set of light, onyx armour.

It wasn't as heavy as the armour that I'd seen the old Demon Queen wear in Maria's memories, or the set Freya had worn when she'd arrived, which had been very similar.

As I looked at it, I realised that most of it was actually black leather, but there were onyx parts covering the most important spots. Notably, there was an onyx breastplate.

"I thought you might need it," Freya said. "You know, in general. You've already gotten into trouble, and the thought of you getting into more without a decent set of armour... Well, I had this made for you. I know that you're a Neutral Witch, but I talked to some friends, and apparently Demon armour is just that good that it tends to be the choice of Neutral beings as well as Dark."

I smiled as I looked it over, Maria's knowledge telling me that it was well-made. "Thank you, Freya. Really. It's beautiful."

Freya shrugged. "I just figured that you might need it, and I had the resources. But this kind of armour will show more than a little respect for Maria tonight."

I nodded, my throat tightening.

"Well," Freya said, placing her hand on my shoulder and squeezing gently, "I'll just wait outside until you're ready."

I nodded again as she left the room before turning to the armour.

Thankfully, Maria's knowledge told me exactly how to put the armour on, as I would have had no idea otherwise.

Natalie looked away, giving me some privacy, which I appreciated, given that the armour was probably too bulky to comfortably take into the bathroom.

After a few minutes, I finally finished strapping on the armour, and I turned to the mirror, looking myself over.

I almost didn't recognise myself in the onyx and dark leather, matching the dark circles under my eyes and bringing out the green in my right one, which I was still getting used to.

I turned to Natalie. "Okay, well, I think I'm ready."

The words were a lie, but I had no idea when I would actually be ready, and waiting seemed somehow worse than just moving forward.

As if stopping would allow everything that had happened not just to catch up with me, but to overwhelm me.

Natalie gave me a soft smile as she looked me over. "You look good. The armour suits you."

Heat rose to my cheeks as I shrugged. "Thanks."

I turned to the door to escape the fluttering in my stomach, dousing it in ice as I refocused on the task before me.

I left the room to see Freya still standing outside.

She also smiled when she saw me. "It looks like the armour fits."

"Yeah," I said. "Thanks."

"Well, like I said, if you're going to get into trouble, I would prefer you're prepared for it. Now, come on. Everyone will be waiting."

I frowned. Who was *everyone*? Charlotte and Lena had said that they would come, but that would be it.

Though, I supposed Freya had maybe asked Damon to also be there. And possibly Mr Stiles, though I doubted he would agree. As much as he was okay with my bond with Maria, she had still tried to kill him.

We headed downstairs to see both Charlotte and Lena waiting for us by the door, wearing similar dresses to Natalie.

"Queen Freya," Charlotte squeaked as soon as she saw her, bowing.

Lena just folded her arms at her girlfriend's display, clearly not interested in showing Freya any respect.

Which was fair, I probably wouldn't either if she wasn't my sister, making me exempt.

Freya smiled. "It's okay, you don't need to bow or anything. You must be Charlotte, right? And Lena?"

Both Charlotte and Lena nodded.

Freya turned to Charlotte. "Have you thought about my offer, Charlotte?"

Charlotte just stared at her. "Your...?"

I stepped in, realising what was happening. "Sorry, Freya, I forgot to mention it to her."

"Of course. Apologies, I shouldn't have expected you to focus on this today." She turned back to Charlotte. "Amy told me that you made a prophecy that seemed to be about her. I was wondering if you would want some help in getting more from your powers as a Seer."

Charlotte shifted her weight awkwardly, twisting a strand of hair between her fingers. "I... To be honest, I don't really use those powers if I can avoid it. A poorly made prophecy is too dangerous. Someone could get hurt."

"All the more reason to have more accurate prophecies, wouldn't you say?"

Charlotte sighed. "I guess... But what about the bad prophecies in the meantime? I can't just take them back."

"No, you can't, but you can be sensible about them. People only get hurt by poorly made prophecies if they take them at face value. And I'm not suggesting you try to prophesize anything at random, just that you dig into this one a little deeper. And if you're likely to get in as much trouble as Amy does, it will probably be good to be able to see what's coming."

"Okay, I guess... I guess a little training couldn't hurt. As long as you don't think the prophecies will hurt anyone."

"I'll make sure of it. You can train with just me, and I already know all of the prophecies about my life. Or at least, I know enough that you couldn't change anything with more details."

Charlotte nodded. "Yeah. Well, okay then."

Freya smiled before turning to the door and heading out.

The rest of us followed, our boots crushing on a thin layer of frost across the ground.

My breath came out in white puffs as I shivered in my armour, the cloudless night sky giving no protection from the frozen air.

Winter had finally come.

We headed towards the woods at the edge of campus, the trees now either completely bare or struggling to hang on to the last few golden leaves of autumn as frost clung to the branches.

My stomach turned with nerves at the reminder of where we were going.

We made our way over, but as we got closer, I saw that there were dozens of specs of light at the tree line.

And then I got closer and realised that it was hundreds.

Hundreds of candles, all held by the other students.

Practically the entire school was there.

What were they all doing there?

Before I could even consider an answer, one of Victoria's friends – whose name I didn't know – came over.

"Hey," she said softly. "Victoria wanted to apologise again. I know that you two haven't been friends in the past, but... Well, we all think that what happened to Maria was messed up. And we all just... None of us thought that we could actually *do* anything. And then Willow did and... Well, we're here because we're sorry. If we'd just done something sooner..."

I just stared at her, unable to comprehend what she was saying.

She stepped back into the crowd.

I turned to Freya, looking for anyone to shed light on this.

She sighed, her lips pulled into a grim line. "The Council thought that killing Maria in front of you all would scare you into compliance. And it might have worked. But you refusing to denounce Maria, and Willow stepping in to save you changed that. They saw that fighting back wasn't hopeless."

I nodded, the explanation making as much sense as anything about this situation did.

"Do you need me to tell you the spell?" Freya asked, and it took me a moment to realise that she was referring to the ritual to put Maria to rest.

"No, it's okay, I've got it."

Freya nodded and I took a deep breath before raising my head as best I could.

I headed through the crowd, forcing my feet to go one after the other, knowing that I had to face what waited for me at the front.

The crowd parted without resistance, allowing me through and to easily reach the endpoint.

The clearing that was connected to Nature.

Not Nature's clearing, but the one that Willow and I had gone to before Nature had opened the doorway to hers.

The clearing where Maria had taken me to find my wand.

Now, the ground was covered in flowers, hundreds of colours all leading up to cover a newly formed mound of earth.

As well as covering the body on top, hiding her from sight, the pattern of the flowers following her features enough to represent what lay beneath.

Maria.

Or what was left of her.

The ritual didn't require the body to be covered, but I was glad that Freya had. I knew that it had been her – the flowers reeked of her magic – and I was grateful.

I wasn't sure I could see Maria like that.

Cold and lifeless.

With the wound she had taken for me.

I turned to the gathered crowd.

Did they even understand what had happened?

"Maria died protecting me," I said, forcing myself to speak up so that everyone could hear me. "She could have escaped. She could have just left. But she came back because the Council had threatened to hurt me, and keep hurting me, until she gave herself up.

"And what for? Why the hell were they so eager to kill her? Because they knew she was powerful and they also knew that she didn't like bullies.

"But more than that, they thought killing her in front of you... In front of me... In front of *us* would scare us into silence. That we, the young Witches more likely to back Esme's vision of the future than theirs, would be cowed by their show of strength. After all, if Maria Brown couldn't defeat them, who could?

"The thing is, Maria was alone. She had me, but no one else in this time knew her beyond what the history books had said about her. The books written by powerful people she'd antagonised.

"Well, I'm also powerful, and I'm not alone, and if the Council thinks that I'm just going to let them get away with this, they've got another think coming."

I wasn't sure what I expected from my impassioned words.

I'd just needed to get them out.

I just needed to have people hear me when I said that I wouldn't let the Council off the hook.

Whether they cared or not...

But then, they were here, weren't they? Why would that be if they didn't care at all?

My eyes were pulled to a flicker of light moving, and I turned to see that Natalie had lit the end of her wand, and was raising it into the air in a deliberate sign of...

What?

Agreement?

Empathy?

Solidarity.

I was sure of the last one as Natalie nodded and Lena and Charlotte also raised their wands.

Most of the crowd were holding candles, so they raised them instead of their wands.

I just watched in awe.

Had Freya been right? Had Willow's attack on the wards to save me shown everyone that fighting the Council wasn't pointless?

That we could actually do this, if we stood together?

I wasn't sure how to respond to that, so I simply took my own wand and turned to the flower-covered figure that used to be Maria.

The words for the spell came to my mind and I spoke them in my mind as I slowly waved my wand over her.

Only, as I cast the spell, I felt not only my magic.

No, Freya's magic joined my own.

I knew that the spell could be done by a group of people, but I'd expected to do it alone.

But Freya's magic was swiftly joined by the familiar feel of Natalie's.

And then Lena's and Charlotte's.

And then more. More magic that I didn't recognise, but each new strand from each new Witch joined the spell in quick succession, until I was humming with Energy from dozens of Witches, if not hundreds.

And it eclipsed Freya.

I never lost the feel of her magic in the spell, as strong and familiar as it was.

But as strong as she was as an Angel, her power didn't come close to that of all of us Witches standing together.

The ground beneath me began to move, drawing my attention back from the feeling, and to the task at hand.

My heart ached in my chest as I realised that this was it.

This was the end.

"Goodbye Maria," I said, my voice cracking, as the mound of earth before me slowly sank to the ground. "I return you to Nature and hope that you find peace."

The flowers flattened to the ground, signalling that Maria had been swallowed by the soil.

A few moments later, a sprout came up from the ground.

It thickened quickly, growing tall enough to tower over us, swiftly developing into the familiar shape of a tree.

A tree that bloomed with more green than I would have thought possible before I'd seen Nature's clearing, a stark contrast to the bare and frozen branches around us.

It seemed that Nature, too, wanted to mark Maria's passing.

And allow something to grow in her wake.

Both exhaustion from the spell and emotional exhaustion overtook me, and I barely registered as others spoke and the crowd finally dispersed.

Natalie placed a hand on my arm, gently guiding me back to the dormitories.

I wanted to argue, to stay here and spend the night in nature, but I didn't have the strength, so I let Natalie guide me.

"Did you feel that?" Lena asked as we walked back, her words the first to cut through my haze. "During the spell, I mean. When all of us put our power together... Maybe if we'd thought to do that with the Council..."

I was glad that she didn't finish the thought, not wanting to face it.

I'd assumed that none of the other students would care about Maria. None of the teachers had, so I'd assumed they wouldn't either.

And maybe they wouldn't have helped before.

Maybe they'd needed to see her blood spilled before they realised just how screwed up the Council was.

Or maybe it hadn't even been that that had changed their minds.

Maybe it had been their threat to kill me. The girl in the same uniform as them.

That thought filled me with rage – Maria had deserved help before that point, and no one else had seen it – but I was too exhausted for that to translate into anything more than bile rising impotently in my stomach.

At least things were finally changing.

I tried to take some comfort in that as Natalie led me up to our room.

I barely managed to get my armour off in my haze, before crawling into bed, glad that Natalie didn't need any verbal prompting to climb in beside me and hold me tight.

Chapter Five

I awoke curled up next to Natalie, but this time, I didn't self-consciously pull away.

No, if she was happy enough with this, then so was I.

Natalie moved as I stirred next to her, turning to face me.

"Hey," she said softly. "How are you doing?"

I groaned. "About as well as I have been for the past few days."

I then sighed as I pushed myself up to a sitting position. "I still don't know what to make of last night, and the fact that everyone was there. I want to believe that it means that everyone's turning against the Council, but..."

"But?"

"I don't want to count my chickens before they've hatched. I can't let the Council get away with killing Maria, Natalie, but they're not just going to take an attack lying down. Everyone might have stood with me last night, but what happens when the danger sets in? I just don't think they'll stick around."

"Maybe not," Natalie said. "But I'm not going anywhere. Don't forget that."

I gave her a small smile. "I won't."

"You know," Natalie said, "if you're not feeling up to it, we don't have to go to class today. I'm sure Ms Griffin would understand."

I bit my lip, sorely tempted by her offer. I knew that there was very little left for me in the classes. Just memorising odd facts for Human tests that would mean nothing to me going forward. Or learning about magic that I already knew about through Maria's memories.

History of Magic might teach me something new, and Maria's knowledge couldn't replace the muscle memory of Magical Self-Defence, but I couldn't see how any of the other classes would be worth my time.

Still, despite how tempting it was to spend all day with Natalie instead, she wasn't in the same position as me.

She would actually get something out of the classes, and I couldn't take her away from them for my own selfish reasons.

"It's probably best to just try to return to normal as best we can," I finally said. "Which means going to classes."

"Okay. If you're sure."

I HAD BEEN RIGHT ABOUT classes not having anything of worth for me, so I just tuned out completely, my thoughts focused more on the one question that had been haunting me since the night before.

Where did I actually go from here?

I wanted to make the Council pay, but... What did that actually look like?

I spent most of the day thinking on that problem, without making much progress.

After all, as much as I knew the Council had to go, there were still plenty of holes in my knowledge of the wider magical world.

Maria had learned a lot, but her focus had always been on finding and freeing her coven. She needed to know enough about the modern magical community to survive, nothing more.

So that was all I knew.

Which meant that I would have to learn more before moving forward.

I left my last class deep in thought, almost running right into Charlotte.

"Hey," she said, twisting at a loose strand of hair. "So... Queen Freya said that I should go and see her after school to get help with training, and I was wondering... Well, she is your-" She cut herself off, presumably remembering that we were in public before saying that Freya was my sister.

She sighed, looking more than a little defeated before finally blurting out, "Would you come with me? I... I'm not good with strangers."

I smiled. "Of course. But why not ask Lena? Not that I mind, just doesn't she normally do things like this with you?"

Charlotte cringed as we turned and headed towards the administration building. "She does, but... Most people can't handle prophecies, Amelia. Knowing the future – even if it's just a possible future – messes with people. They can't let go of it, and they usually tie themselves in knots trying to either make it come true or avoid it, and that often changes their fate anyway. If I do this... Lena is my Soulbound. Our fates are tied together, so if I'm practicing my Seer skills..."

"You'll likely see her future?"

Charlotte nodded. "And I don't think she can handle it. I mean, I love Lena with everything I have, but... Well, she's not the best at compartmentalising. She would never be able to leave it alone. I can't do that to her."

"It's okay," I said. "I don't mind, I was just curious."

Charlotte continued to twist at her hair. "I wish that things were different. Either that I could have her there with me, or that I didn't need someone to hold my hand so often..."

"It's understandable that she can't be here," I said before shrugging. "And it's understandable that you don't want to see Freya alone. She would intimidate anyone, not just a Litcorde. And she'll understand if I come. I mean, isn't she Litcorde as well?"

"You ask that as if she wasn't your- As if you don't have more reason to know than me."

I shrugged again. "I don't think she ever told our parents or me. I don't know if she just found out later, or..."

"Or if it's something you don't tell adoptive parents, in case they decide you're not worth the hassle?"

I winced at the thought. "I can't imagine any parents just abandoning their child over something like that, adopted or not."

Charlotte sighed. "I wish I could tell you that it was uncommon. But I guess Litcorde are just too much for some people..."

"Well, those people are assholes."

Charlotte managed a small smile at that as we reached the administration building, but it was clear that it was strained.

I led her through the building and down the stairs, finding Freya's room and knocking on the door.

"Come in," Freya called from beyond.

Charlotte tensed beside me and I offered her an understanding smile. "She won't bite."

Charlotte managed another strained smile and a nod, and I figured that was the best I was going to get from her as I opened the door to Freya's room.

Freya and Damon were both inside, and as we entered, I saw a small head pop up over Damon's shoulders.

Katherine.

Charlotte twisted at her hair, her fingers moving faster than before.

"Hey," I said as I closed the door behind us. "Charlotte is here for her Seer training."

Before Freya could respond, Katherine spoke up, "Auntie Amy! Mum said I could look around the school if you took me."

Freya placed a gentle hand on her daughter's shoulder. "I didn't say that, I said that it was too dangerous for you to go wandering alone."

"I won't be alone if Auntie Amy is with me!"

Freya shook her head.

Katherine just continued on. "Can I come here when I'm older? I want to go to school with everyone."

"No, Katherine. The school only teaches Witches at the moment, and even if they open up to other species, you need to stay at home and learn with other Demons."

Katherine pouted and I wondered if she knew what Freya had shared with me.

That she would never develop magic.

She was too young right now to break through, so it was entirely possible that she just didn't know that it wasn't going to happen.

After all, she was young to be keeping a secret like that.

Or maybe she did know, but still wanted to be as much a part of the magical world as anyone else.

"But perhaps Dad can show you around for now," Freya continued. "Charlotte's going to need some privacy for this."

Damon nodded before heading for the door, Katherine still on his shoulders. "Come on, let's go and find Uncle Aaron."

Charlotte bit her lip as she turned back to Freya. "I wouldn't have minded if they stayed."

Freya smiled. "As much as you might not have, I don't think Katherine is old enough to really deal with learning about her future just yet."

"Okay, yeah, that makes sense."

"The exercises Alice gave me to practice with you shouldn't mean looking too far into the future, but it's best to be safe." Freya then turned to me. "I understand if you want Amelia here while we train, but it might mean that you focus on her future."

Charlotte nodded, though didn't answer.

"I don't mind staying," I said.

But then Charlotte sighed. "No, I... It's okay. I'll be okay."

"Are you sure?" I asked and Charlotte nodded.

"Yeah, I am. It's okay, Amelia. Thanks for bringing me here, at least."

"It was no problem," I said before heading out of her room.

I paused for a moment before making my way to Mr Stiles' room, wondering if he was available for some combat training.

But when I got there, I saw that he and Damon were playing with Katherine, and I didn't have the heart to interrupt.

So, I headed to the dining room to get something to eat, before heading back to my room for the night.

NATALIE CAUGHT UP WITH me in the dining hall, and we ate together before heading back to our room.

As we walked, we passed a couple holding hands and my stomach twisted as my thoughts turned to Willow.

I pulled out my phone and attempted to send her another text.

I got the same response as before.

I turned back to Natalie to see her giving me a sympathetic look. "Tried to text Willow again?"

"Yep."

"Still no response?"

I sighed. "It's still just the same as before. No real response from her..."

"Well, if she's with her father and the *Fin'Hathan*, that makes sense."

"I know, I just... I wish I knew for sure that she was okay. That she was safe and okay with everything that happened. Not that she should be okay with it, just... " I sighed once more, this time drawing it out as I let my head roll back for a moment before bringing it back to face

Natalie. "I wish that if she wasn't okay, I was with her, you know? That she wasn't alone. And I know that she's not really alone if she's with her father, but..."

"But you still wish you were with her?"

I nodded. "I wish that she were here with me, so... If she feels the same way, then she might wish that I were with her, and I'm not, and that... I wish things were different."

"I know. But hopefully, she won't be gone for long."

"Yeah," I said, knowing that Willow had seemed more than capable before she'd left. Her father had trained her well, and maybe that meant that she just needed to take one final step before becoming *Fin'Hathan*.

Maybe that meant that she didn't have to be gone for too long...

But then there was that question of what that final step might be, and I quickly pushed away that thought as my stomach churned, less than eager to find the answer.

I wished that Willow could have told me more before leaving. Even the idea that she might be with the *Fin'Hathan* was just a guess on my part.

There hadn't exactly been time, and I wasn't sure that even Willow had been sure of her destination.

But still, anything would have been better than this silence.

As we reached our room, I quickly got changed into my pyjamas, feeling more than a little exhausted.

Natalie did the same and slipped into my bed next to me as I brought out my laptop and loaded up a game of Civ.

"Are you sure you're okay with this?" I asked once we were several turns into the game. "Staying with me at night, I mean. I know that there's not much room."

Natalie gave me a small smile, placing a reassuring hand on my arm. "I'm sure that I don't mind, Amy. I know that losing your connection to Maria was hard, and any kind of connection I can give to make up for it... Well, I know that you would prefer Willow if she were here, but I can be here for now."

"No," I said firmly. "It's different because we're friends, not dating, but that doesn't mean that I would *prefer* either one of you."

I leaned into her to punctuate my words, and while Natalie didn't respond, she also didn't pull away, just taking her next turn in the game and letting my words linger between us, anything else remaining unsaid.

Chapter Six

The next day, I checked out of most of my lessons once again, still not sure what I was going to do, but knowing that it had to be something.

I spent most of the day in the kind of daze I hadn't felt since before I'd started my ADHD medication.

But then it was the last lesson, and I headed to the gym feeling a little better.

Combat training was something I still needed to practice, after all.

And it was something I would likely need.

I got changed quickly before heading through to the gym, only to frown as I arrived to see not just Ms Espina there, but also Freya and Damon.

Everyone else seemed just as confused by their appearance as I was, the room filled with hushed voices as everyone did a bad job of trying not to stare.

"All right, girls," Ms Espina said once we were all in the room, quieting the chatter. "We've got two special guests here with us today. The intention in this class is to teach you as many forms of combat as possible, and as we have experts in Demonic martial arts here, I thought they could show you girls a few things. And they have agreed to give a demonstration, and then help you to learn some of the basics."

She then turned to Freya and Damon. "I'll pass the lesson over to you now."

Damon was the one to nod in response before stepping forward. "Good afternoon, girls. You probably know me as Queen Freya's Consort, but I'm also the Head of her Queensguard, which means that I'm in charge of training all of her guards.

"Now, I believe Ms Espina promised you a demonstration." He turned to Freya. "Mind helping me with this?"

She smiled. "Not at all." She then turned to the rest of us. "Keep your attention on Damon if you want to learn proper Demon technique. My style is a bit more... haphazard."

Damon grinned at that as Ms Espina motioned for everyone to give Damon and Freya more room than most people would possibly need.

But we were talking about two of the most powerful beings in existence.

Freya was the only Angel of Life in existence, and the information I'd read on Freya said that Damon was one of the most powerful Demons in the Underworld.

Freya set her right foot back, raising her arms in a defensive position, ready for a strike.

Damon took just a moment before moving faster than any of us could see, rushing forward to strike at his wife.

Freya met his speed, however, her hand coming up to deflect his strike.

That was the last thing I could see clearly, Damon and Freya both moving faster than I could track, even when I fuelled my magic into my eyesight, trying to speed it up as fast as I could.

Eventually, with enough magic, I started to catch up just enough to make out the two figures. Neither of their details were distinct, but I got the general gist.

And Freya hadn't been kidding when she'd said that her technique was haphazard. She didn't really seem all that preoccupied in deflecting Damon's strikes. No, she deflected the worst of his blows, but she just absorbed most of them.

And while Damon flinched when she struck him, his strikes seemed to do nothing to her.

I wondered if that was one of the perks of being an Angel. An enhanced stamina to rival no other.

Or maybe she was just so used to pain that it didn't even register for her.

My stomach twinged at the thought, but it wasn't just with sympathy.

No, it was empathy.

I knew that feeling all too well at this point.

After all of the pain the Council had put me through, would anything of the kind bother me again?

I almost wished that it would. As impractical as it would be – especially if I was determined to fight the Council – I didn't want them to have scarred me so.

I didn't want them to have taken anything so fundamental from me.

But I couldn't escape the creeping suspicion that they had.

That I'd changed in their dungeon, in ways that I couldn't yet fully comprehend.

In ways that I might never recover from.

Bile rose in my stomach at the thought and it took everything I had to keep it down as wind whipped through my hair, and a moment later, Damon lost his footing.

Freya had used her control over the elements to knock him back.

She easily knocked him to the ground after that, though she looked slightly sheepish.

"Sorry. I know this was supposed to be a demonstration of Demonic fighting styles only, but I'm so used to relying on my elemental magic, it's hard to turn it off in a fight."

Damon just smiled as he turned back to me and my fellow students. "Well, this was just supposed to be a demonstration, I'm not expecting anyone in the class to be able to emulate either of us today, never mind take on an Angel. I just wanted to show you all what's possible if you commit yourself to training.

"Now, let's go slow and show you all some of the basic forms."

Damon turned back to Freya, though this time he kept his moves slow and deliberate.

Freya also turned to face him, mirroring his movements and speed.

They then moved through several basic forms, Damon narrating both of their movements as they went.

After just a few moves, he turned back to us. "All right, let's see you all try to replicate that. And don't worry if you can't do it perfectly right away. You'll be using muscles here that I imagine most of you haven't had a need to train, even if you regularly exercise."

I nodded, vaguely remembering when I'd first started Taekwondo. I'd been a fairly active child, but it had still taken a while to get used to using my muscles in ways I hadn't before.

But given that experience, I doubted these simple forms were going to cause me much trouble.

I moved through them as Damon made his way around the room, not struggling to physically replicate anything I'd seen, but wondering if I'd managed to remember exactly what I was supposed to be doing accurately.

As Damon made his way slowly around the room, Freya made her way over to me and smiled as she looked over my technique.

"Well, looks like you picked this up fast."

"It's not that hard if you've had martial arts training before."

"I guess not." She shrugged. "I wouldn't know, I hadn't so much as thrown a proper punch before my first real fight. I had to learn quickly and mostly on my own."

I sighed. "You know, the annoying thing is that I haven't actually been given the chance to fight most of the shit I've had to deal with. The Amazons put me through trials, and I was stupid enough to believe the Council's lies when they said that they would let me go. I was stupid enough to think that I could out smart them. So, when it came time to fight... They had me shackled, unable to do anything."

Dark Energy crackled across my skin as Freya gave me a sympathetic look.

"I wouldn't wish the fights I had on anyone," Freya eventually said. "But the ones that hurt the most – that took the most from me – weren't ones that I could physically fight either."

"Is there any way to prepare for that kind of fight?"

Freya shook her head. "Not that I've ever found. Just... keep your friends close. They might be the thing that saves you."

I nodded as I continued to go through the moves.

"Perhaps we should move on to something more difficult," Freya said. "Though I'm not as well-versed as Damon at this kind of thing."

I relaxed my stance and turned to her properly. "Actually, I was wondering, could you maybe help me with the magic Nature awoke in me? I mean, I'm supposed to be powerful, right? But no one has been able to really teach me how to *use* any of my power. No one but..."

Freya gave me a sympathetic look. "But Maria?"

I nodded as I realised that she'd cast a privacy spell, keeping our words between just us. "She was Angelborn as well. But... There wasn't enough time to learn everything. She passed on her knowledge, but she didn't have elemental abilities."

"Yeah, I guess most Angelborn are born from just Angels of Life, whereas I'm one of Nature's daughters as well."

I wondered if there had ever been an Angelborn like me before.

My throat tightened at the lonely thought as my hand instinctively went to my cheek, just beneath my wild green eye.

"I don't know what I am now," I confessed. "Nature said that she just awoke the power that you gave me, but... Does that make me a Witch still, or something else?"

Freya sighed. "In my experience? It doesn't matter. The Demons were happy to claim me because I was a Dark Angel and the daughter of their King. But before that? Who the hell knows what I am, Amy. People say 'Angel' or 'Queen' because it's easiest, but that's not even half the story. I've had so many titles and nicknames over the years, even I forget them all.

"Your people are whoever will accept you. And if no one does, then you make your own."

It sounded so simple when she put it like that, but I knew first-hand that it wasn't.

"You've got your friends here," Freya said and I realised that my thoughts must have been evident on my features. "That's a start. Trust me, I know it's not easy, but... It's possible. And there are more than a few days that I miss living on Earth with my rag-tag group of friends."

I nodded, but decided that I wanted to talk about something – anything – else.

Something less exhausting...

Thankfully, Freya said, "So, about these elemental powers. Have you ever been able to use magic without a spell?"

"I can create raw Energy and I can shift."

"Anything else?"

I shook my head. "No, everything else has been through my wand."

"That makes sense, given that you're a Witch. My elemental powers just come to me." She raised her hand and flame engulfed it for a moment before dissipating. "But you likely need a spell. Has there been an element that you've been particularly drawn to? Anything that calls to you over the others?"

"Not really. But then, if I need a spell, I probably won't know until I experiment."

"True. Well, given your current mental state, I would suggest starting with fire. Do you know one to produce flames?"

I searched through Maria's knowledge in my mind, finding the spell in question before nodding.

Freya looked around, and I realised that she was checking that no one was near us before she said, "Okay, well, give it a go, and let's see what you can do."

I frowned. My wand was with my belongings back in the changing room.

But as soon as that thought came to me, my wand shifted to my hand.

Or, I guess I shifted it.

I was so used to having it on me, I didn't notice it anymore, but when I realised it wasn't in my hand... It was like a part of me was missing...

Which I suppose is why I was able to so easily shift it back to me.

I focused on the spell from Maria's knowledge, funnelling my magic through my wand.

Fire erupted from the end of my wand before looping back to snake around my arm, wrapping around me and keeping me safe from anything that might try to get past it.

Freya then smiled as I put away my wand, the fire remaining, and she reached her arm out towards the door.

I wasn't sure what was happening, and then a stream of water flew through the door, wrapping around Freya much as the fire had wrapped around me, presumably pulled from the slush and rain water covering the school grounds.

Freya then readied herself into a defensive posture. "Ready to go through those moves again, but this time against an opponent?"

I nodded, taking the rest of my magic and using it to charge my muscles, knowing that I would need the extra strength and speed to even hope to spar with Freya, even if she took it easy on me.

Freya struck first, but it was more than simple for me to repeat my earlier moves, bringing my hand up to block hers.

The fire and water clashed in a hiss of steam and I felt a pull on my magical reserves as the fire that had been extinguished sought to renew itself.

I allowed the fire to pull from what remained of my magic as I realised that Freya wasn't pulling more water from outside.

Which meant that I just had to keep this up until she ran out.

Freya struck once more, and I managed to block her again before daring a strike of my own.

Freya blocked me with ease and we entered a dance of blows and blocks, neither of us managing to get the upper hand on the other.

My breath turned to laboured pants as a familiar, soul-deep exhaustion told me that I was pushing my magic to my limits.

But Freya still seemed to have the same amount of water.

How? I was constantly evaporating it into the air of the gym.

The *dry* air.

Shit. She was pulling the water back out of the air, reforming it into a liquid.

I would have probably been impressed if the room wasn't starting to spin.

A moment later, a torrent of water dropped from above, drenching me and extinguishing the flames in their entirety, putting an end to the spell.

"Sorry," Freya said as I looked up at her through the soaked strands of my hair that were now forming a platinum blonde curtain over my eyes. "You looked like you were about to pass out."

I nodded, not sure that I had the strength for words as the room continued to spin slightly, and I struggled to keep my lunch down.

Freya shifted a bottle of Lucozade to her hand before passing it to me. "Here, you need to replenish... Well, everything."

I nodded, taking the bottle and clumsily struggling to remove the cap. Once I finally had it off, I let it drop to the floor as I downed the contents of the bottle.

When I was done, the room was spinning less and I was a little more in control of my stomach.

"I think we should call it a day at that," Freya said. "But you did well. You held out for much longer than I expected you to, and you'll only get better with time. Magic is like a muscle. The more you use it, the better you'll get."

I grimaced. "I ran out of time weeks ago."

Freya, thankfully, didn't try to argue, just placing her hand on my shoulder, her familiar magic giving me some small relief. "I know. But late is better than never."

I nodded, but my stomach twisted.

That thought wasn't much solace for Maria, was it?

I pushed my hair back out of my face, only to frown as I caught someone looking at me out of the corner of their eye.

As soon as I turned to them, they turned away, but I scanned the room and found almost every student doing a terrible job of pretending not to watch me and Freya.

I suppressed a sigh. I couldn't exactly blame them – I'd probably have done the same in their place – but I wasn't sure that I wanted people watching me train with elemental magic.

Just one more thing reminding them that I was different.

I shouldn't care. I'd spent my entire life being different.

But not here.

No one had known that I was the weird kid when I first came to Ember Academy.

But that had probably been thrown out the window when I'd helped Maria on Samhain, if I was being honest with myself.

"Go and get dressed," Freya said. "Then we can see about getting you some food."

I nodded before heading off to the changing rooms and getting back into my uniform as quickly as I could manage, exhaustion making my hands sluggish.

Eventually, I made it out of the building to find Freya waiting for me, and snow falling.

"Huh," I said as I looked up at the soft flakes floating to the ground. "I can't remember the last time I saw real snow."

Freya grimaced. "Yeah, climate change will do that. But I was getting sick of the sleet and sludge."

"You're doing this?"

She nodded. "Yeah. It's strange, being on Earth. In the Underworld, I don't have the same connection to everything that I do here. If I'm not careful here, the weather will just turn into a constant reflection of my mood. And I... Well, I would become a reflection in turn. The Earth is screaming, and if I'm not careful, I'll become the avatar of that scream."

"Yeah, Nature mentioned something about her Daughters not being able to handle the strain of the Earth burning, and that you dealt with it by staying in the Underworld."

Freya sighed. "It used to not be so bad, but after I shed my humanity... Well, it was almost unbearable until my heartbond cast a spell that connected the two of us through our shared elemental powers, grounding me more while I'm here."

Before I could figure out what to ask next without overstepping, one of Freya's guards approached.

He bowed, but just barely. A formality that he had to go through with, but knew her too well for, I would guess. "Queen Freya. We found the woman you were looking for. She's waiting for you in your room."

Freya turned to me. "Well, you probably still need food, but if Maureen is here, I assume you'll want to join me in speaking to her?"

I hesitated, remembering that I hadn't told Freya everything that had happened with Maureen.

Like that she had betrayed me...

But I nodded. I had suggested that Freya bring her, and I had to admit, I was curious to know what had happened to her.

We headed back to the administration building, my heart thundering with every step.

I didn't know why. Maureen had been the one to betray me, I should be angry, not nervous.

It wasn't as if she could hurt me again. Not here, with Freya to protect me.

But still, as we reached the door to Freya's room, I reflexively grabbed my wand and cast a glamour over myself, turning myself invisible before Freya could open the door enough for anyone inside to see me.

Freya turned to me – or where I had just been from her perspective – and raised an eyebrow, but she didn't attempt to question me.

She just turned back to the room.

And the woman pacing within.

"Queen Freya," Maureen squeaked as she turned to see her before bowing. "I... One of your guards came to find me. He said that I wasn't in trouble, but wouldn't explain more about why you wanted to see me."

"I apologise if that made you nervous," Freya said and Maureen finally straightened her back, only to bring her hand to her mouth, her other hand holding her wrist. Restraining her nails from getting near her teeth.

Freya gave her a kind smile. "Though I am curious why you agreed to come if you're so nervous."

Maureen glanced away. "I almost didn't. But Caroline convinced me, so here I am. If a woman you exiled thinks it's safe to meet you, it probably is."

Freya's smile took on a bittersweet edge. "Yes, well, I should probably stop keeping you in suspense. I heard about your predicament. That you're a Guide, pregnant with a child sired by a Demon. I can sense the life within you. It's struggling, and I do not think it will win the fight. Not without help. Thankfully, Angels of Life are powerful healers. I can help you, if you want."

Maureen just stared at her for several moments.

And then tears poured down her cheeks in silent torrents.

She clumsily attempted to wipe them away before turning back to Freya. "I... Why would you help? I mean, I'm not a Demon, and you don't know me."

"You might not be a Demon, but your child is on its father's side. That makes it my responsibility as Queen to help both of you."

Maureen shook her head with a wet sound of dismissal. "I don't buy that. You're the Queen of the Underworld. This is something for a healer, not a queen."

Freya gave a half-shrug. "You're right. I do try to help as many people as possible, but this is going to be a taxing feat even for me, and I doubt I would have even heard about it if someone who means a lot to me hadn't asked me to help you."

Maureen frowned. "Someone asked you to help? Who? No one's supposed to know about the child." She then sighed. "Though I wouldn't be shocked if Caroline and Persephone had figured it out. Especially Persephone... But you exiled them. You're not supposed to have contact with them anymore."

"And as far as anyone knows, I don't," Freya said, her voice almost scarily firm.

Maureen nodded swiftly. "Of course. I won't tell anyone. I swear."

I cringed. I wasn't sure that we could trust Maureen to keep her word, and she only thought that Caroline had been the one to tell Freya because I'd glamoured myself, and Freya had presumably taken that to mean that I didn't want her to tell Maureen that I had been the one to ask for this.

And I didn't, but I also didn't want to cause trouble for Freya...

"You might want to sit down," Freya said, gently moving Maureen over to one of the chairs in the corner of the room. "I'm not exactly sure how this will work, but it will take a lot of magic."

Maureen raised an eyebrow. "You're not sure how it will work? Isn't it just part of your healing powers?"

"Well, yes, technically, but the best way to do this will be to strengthen your child by imbuing it with my magic. That's not something I regularly do."

Maureen frowned. "Someone must have really called in a favour for me…"

Freya smiled. "Not really. Like I said, they mean a lot to me, so this wasn't that big of an ask."

I couldn't help but smile, my throat tightening at Freya's words.

I'd recommended this as a way to get information on the Council, but this was a big ask. Maybe Freya wouldn't have done it if anyone else had asked.

I was gripped by the sudden urge to rush forward and hug my sister tight, but I restrained myself, not wanting to interrupt.

"All right," Freya said, moving her hand over to Maureen's abdomen. "Just sit still."

Maureen nodded, her hands going to the arms of her chair, gripping them tight.

There was silence for several moments, and Maureen frowned slightly, biting her lip in what was probably an attempt to stop herself from asking Freya if it was working.

But then, a soft white glow appeared over Freya's hand, slowly spreading up her arm, to her shoulder and neck.

As the glow travelled down to her back, it grew brighter, stretching out behind her to form two large wings made of brilliant white light.

I had to look away as the light engulfed both Freya and Maureen, almost bright enough to be blinding.

But then the light faded, and I looked back as Freya collapsed onto her knees.

"Freya!" I cried, my glamour lapsing as I rushed over to make sure that she was okay, Maureen's presence forgotten.

"I'm okay, Amy," Freya managed as I helped her to a sitting position on the floor. She looked even paler than usual, and was clearly putting effort into controlling her breathing, taking slow and deep breaths. "Just... It took a lot out of me."

"Wait... *Amelia?!*"

I turned to see Maureen staring at me, disbelieving.

Though her attention on me was short-lived, her hand going to her abdomen as she looked down.

"How does the child feel now?" Freya managed to ask, her voice croaking slightly.

"Good. They feel good. They feel a lot stronger now than before." She turned to me. "But... Is it real or is this just a trap? I should have known when they brought me to Ember Academy, but... Why would you be involved in helping me, Amelia? After what I did..."

I shrugged. "I wouldn't wish your situation on anyone, not even my worst enemy. And even if you haven't acted perfectly in the past... Well, I figure we have a worse enemy in common."

"My mother?"

I nodded. "You know that she only let you go because she thought that you were going to lose the child. If you don't..."

Maureen groaned. "You did this to give me a reason to stop her."

"No, I asked Freya to help because she could and it was the right thing to do. You can leave now if you want. And even if you don't, your mother didn't seem to be keeping you in the loop, so there's every chance that you don't know anything that could help."

Maureen grimaced. "You're not wrong that she keeps me at a distance. But... Well, I've been doing some digging, trying to figure out how to escape her once and for all." She turned to Freya. "I got some info out of some Slayers. The Council aren't happy that they were sent away from the school, and they're setting some kind of trap. If I were to guess, I'd say that it was a trap for you."

Freya sighed as she tried to get to her feet. I offered my hand and she took it, finally managing to get upright.

"Thank you, Maureen. I'm quite exhausted, but if you tell Dex what you know, he'll be able to confirm the information with my people, and it will hopefully give us the edge we need."

Maureen nodded. "Of course. And if you need anything else..."

"I'll let you know, but it sounds as if you'd be safest kept out of this fight and away from your mother. If you need any help with that, just let me know."

"Thank you, Queen Freya, but I think Caroline has me covered."

Freya smiled. "I don't doubt it. Dex should be two doors down to the left."

Freya indicated to the door and Maureen nodded before heading out, closing the door behind her.

Freya collapsed onto her bed with a groan before pulling out her phone. "Well, that was exhausting," she managed. "If I text Damon and tell him to bring food here, do you want to stay and have some, or do you want to go and eat with your friends? Classes should be over by now."

"I'll stay," I said, and Freya responded by patting the bed next to her.

I took the invitation to sit down, glad for the rest, given my own magical exhaustion.

Freya pushed her pillows up to prop herself into a sitting position before turning to me. "So, what was all that with Maureen?"

I sighed. "Did I tell you that she was in the next cell over from me when the Council had me locked up?"

"No, you did not."

"Well, she was. She couldn't sense a magical signature for the child yet, so her mother locked her up until she could be sure she wasn't pregnant. Apparently, her mother was likely the one who killed her partner after she realised that Maureen had been pregnant before, and was determined that it wouldn't happen again."

"But she escaped?"

"Yeah. She didn't know that I was tied to Maria Brown and that was why I was locked up. But she did know that I had a mentor who I was tied to because Maria would heal me when I saw her in my dreams. So, when her mother asked for information on me in exchange for letting her go once Maureen could sense a magical signature... Well, she didn't know that the information would be the death sentence for Maria that it turned out to be."

"Maybe not, but she must have known that her mother didn't have good intentions when it came to you."

"I know."

"But you still asked me to help her? Even though you had no way of knowing if she would help us in turn?"

I shrugged. "I couldn't just let her be hurt, you know?"

At that, Freya leaned over and wrapped her arms around me. "I know. And I might not be allowed to say this, given how I left, but I'm going to say it anyway; I'm so proud of you, Amy."

I just snuggled into her, grateful that she'd decided to say the words aloud.

I hadn't realised just how much I needed them...

Chapter Seven

Damon arrived not much later, with both Katherine and several bags of fast food.

Freya wolfed down three burgers before I had time to blink, and then downed a large coke.

Though, in her defence, I wasn't much better, quickly inhaling a dozen mozzarella sticks to combat my own magical exhaustion.

"Busy day?" Damon asked.

"I think I just made another Angelborn," Freya told him between bites of her fourth burger.

Damon raised an eyebrow. "Is this for that Maureen woman? I know you said that you might, but..."

"She would have lost the child if I hadn't. I couldn't say no."

There was a look of understanding and heart-breaking sorrow that passed between them at that.

Even Katherine must have noticed, as she placed a comforting hand on Freya's.

Freya responded by lifting her daughter into her lap and holding her close.

Damon eventually nodded, accepting Freya's explanation without further argument. "Does she have the help and resources she's going to need to keep an Angelborn safe?"

"She said Caroline will help her, so I'm going to assume so."

That seemed to be good enough for Damon as we settled into finishing up the rest of the food, Freya and I making quick work of anything in front of us.

Several moments after we'd finished, as we were picking up and clearing away the wrappers, there was a knock at the door.

"Come in," Freya said as she turned to the door.

The guard from earlier – Dex – entered the room. "My Queen, I've finished talking with Maureen and I reached out to our contacts. Esme responded by arriving at the school. She's waiting for you in the infirmary."

Freya frowned. "Any reason for her hurry?"

"She says that she has information you might want."

Freya sighed. "Well, then, I guess I'd better go and talk to her." She turned to me. "You coming? This is probably about the Council."

I nodded, getting to my feet and straightening my jacket. "Yeah, of course."

Freya turned to leave the room and I followed as we headed across the now-dark school grounds, the orbs of light around the school paths the only light, dark clouds obscuring the sky.

It was no longer snowing, and I pulled my jacket tight around me to ward off the biting wind.

Eventually, Freya and I reached the infirmary, finding it empty except for Esme and Sarah.

Freya nodded to both of them before turning her attention to Esme, though she spoke with her hands as well as her mouth so that Sarah could still understand. "Dex tells me you've got some information for me?"

Esme sighed, copying Freya's use of sign language. "He said that you had information on a potential trap the Council are setting."

"Yes, we do. Why?"

"Because I received similar information, but it seemed to come from Amazons who used to work for Dana. I believe in forgiveness, but... Well, I have worried that the information itself might not be accurate. But if you have corroboration..."

Freya turned to me. "What do you think? Do you think Maureen's information might be a trap in and of itself?"

I shrugged, feeling a little awkward that I didn't know how to sign. "I don't see how," I said, and as I spoke, Esme signed to Sarah, presumably relaying my words. "As far as the Council are concerned, Maureen betrayed me. Why give her false information to pass on to me or you? From their perspective, we probably never would have talked again. I'd get it if it was a trap for the Guardians, but if this trap is for you..."

Freya nodded before turning back to Esme. "Amy is right. Unless the Council have the help of an Oracle, I doubt they would have planted this information with our source. They have no idea we're in contact and would have assumed that we were enemies."

Esme smiled. "Well, that's a relief." She turned to Sarah. "I told you that working with at least some of Dana's people would be better than trying to mitigate the fallout from a full-blown purge. We have to show that we're willing to work together."

Sarah didn't look convinced, though she settled for saying, "Well, the information does definitely seem to line up. Though we should perhaps start with the listening post she also told us about, to make sure that her information's correct."

Freya raised an eyebrow. "Listening post?"

Esme sighed as she turned to her. "Apparently, the Council have set up a post in the forest beyond the school's wards. It's about a mile to the south, and they're monitoring all communications in and out of the school. Your man was smart to portal written, encrypted information to me, but anything beyond your heavily secure system will be caught by them. We had intended to tell Gail so that she could handle it, but given that I've made the trip already, I would like to see it for myself."

Freya bit her lip. "I would say that I could go, but going into battle on Earth might loosen my tie to my heartbond, and my humanity."

"You shouldn't go anyway, Queen Freya. And neither should any of the Demons. The Council are probably looking for any excuse to label you as an aggressor and justify a war. Let's not give them the ammunition."

I bit my lip before forcing myself to speak up. "I could go."

Esme turned to me. "Amelia, this will likely be a dangerous fight-"

Freya cut her off. "Amy can handle it, especially if she has her friends with her. And this is her fight as much as anyone's."

"She's still just a student."

"A student the Council have in their sights. Better that she gets small missions in as practice, rather than being thrown in the deep end when the Council finally decide to come for her."

Esme sighed before turning to me. "All right. See if your friends want to come along, and we'll leave in the morning."

I nodded before heading out of the room, pulling my phone out to message my friends.

CHARLOTTE AND LENA were already in my room when I arrived, both of them, and Natalie, in their pyjamas. Charlotte and Lena were sitting on Natalie's bed, but Natalie was sitting on mine.

"So," Lena said, "what's up? Why was your message all cryptic?"

"Because the Council have a listening post outside of the school and they're keyed in to all communications."

Lena frowned. "Even phones? It's hard to get magic to work with tech unless you're a Dwarf. They must really think they're going to overhear something good."

"Well, good or not, Esme's here and she's going to go and take down the post tomorrow. I'm going with her, and any of you can come as well, if you want."

Lena grinned. "Well, I'm definitely going." She turned to Charlotte. "What about you, Lottie? Up for an adventure?"

Charlotte nodded. "Yeah, okay."

I turned to Natalie and she gave me a small smile. "Of course I'm coming with you."

I returned her smile as I went to sit next to her.

Lena nudged Charlotte gently with her elbow. "So, if we're going on a mission, maybe it's time for you to finally use those Seer powers Queen Freya's been helping you with."

Charlotte gave a nervous shrug. "I mean, I've only had one training session with her."

"Yeah, but you said that you managed to make a coherent prophecy without getting drunk."

"'Coherent' is maybe an overstatement. It stayed on the topic I was trying to see things about, at least, but it was still a rambling mess. And I wasn't strictly sober, Queen Freya just gave me a potion that Seers often use to get the same effect I was getting from alcohol."

"But she gave you more, didn't she? And if you stayed on topic, you can look into the future to see what will happen on the mission without worrying that you'll see anything else, right?"

Charlotte sighed.

I leaned forward. "You don't have to if you don't want to. Really, it's not necessary."

"No, I know, but... If I can see the future, maybe I can see what's going to happen and avoid anything bad happening."

"Okay, but only if you're sure."

Charlotte nodded before shifting a small vial of silver liquid to her hand. "This is the potion Queen Freya gave me. Once I take it... Well, my powers can be overwhelming. You're not likely to get anything but prophecy out of me until the effects wear off."

"It's okay," Lena told her, putting a gentle hand on her arm. "We've got you."

Charlotte smiled slightly before knocking back the contents of the vial.

As she brought her head back down, her gaze was unfocused and distant, and when she next spoke, her words were emotionless and detached.

"The snakes are swarming," she said and I shivered, pulling my knees to my chest.

"The snakes are swarming, and full of poison. Fangs piercing many, and pillars will fall. The wind carries change, but not soon enough.

"Poison pierces frozen blood and the Vampire will fall, only to rise again, bound by blood and pain to the Angelborn.

"History repeats, round and round, and pain and blood will heal the rift, and the Angelborn will fall so that the Witches can rise."

Charlotte's gaze then refocused as she slumped forward slightly and Lena's hands went to her shoulders, keeping her upright.

Ice crept down my spine.

The Vampire will fall.

She'd meant Natalie, hadn't she? So, what? Was Natalie going to be hurt? Or worse...

The prophecy was far from clear, but it wasn't something we could risk.

"Guys," Lena said, drawing my attention to the fact that Charlotte was clutching her head, rocking back and forth slightly.

"I'm fine," Charlotte managed. "Just... It's hard to refocus on the present."

Lena gave me and Natalie an apologetic look. "I think we should head back to our room. And... I'm sorry. This probably wasn't the best idea. It didn't really help, did it?"

"It's okay," I said. "It was worth a shot."

Lena nodded before shifting out with Charlotte.

I sighed, running my hand through my hair as I turned back to Natalie.

"She said the old prophecy again," Natalie said, and I nodded, not having missed it.

"We still can't be sure that we're the Vampire and Angelborn." My words lacked conviction and the look Natalie gave me said that I hadn't convinced her.

"And she said that the Angelborn will fall. What do you think that means?"

I shrugged. "I don't know. And if it means something bad... Well, maybe focusing on it will only make it worse."

"Maybe. Or maybe... Maybe we should try to stop the rest of the prophecy?"

"The rest of it?"

"The part that says that we're supposed to be bound together. Amy, maybe we were wrong to say that we could... That we could get as close as we have been without there being risk." She sighed, looking away. "You still love Willow, Amy, and I... I don't want to ruin that in any way."

"You can't," I said firmly. "You can't ruin it because I will always love Willow."

"And that's what makes this so difficult," Natalie turned back to me and I saw that her fangs were fully visible. "The prophecy says that we're supposed to be bound by blood. That can only mean one thing, Amy. The bond forms when a Vampire bites someone. Do you know how *difficult* it is to hear a prophecy say that you're supposed to form that bond – a bond that is supposed to save you somehow – with someone who is in love with someone else?"

My insides churned, my thoughts turning to static as I struggled to accept the implication of what she was saying.

Eventually, "You were the one to push me away," blurted from my mouth, impulsivity the only thing left to give me function. "You want to talk about difficult? What about the woman who keeps pushing you away telling you that, no, now she would want to bond with you, and the fact that you moved on – *after she pushed you away* – is what's making it difficult for her."

"That's not what I said!"

"Then what did you say? What is the point? If you don't want to bond with me – if you don't want to be with me – why do you care about the prophecy or that I'm with Willow?"

Natalie didn't respond and silence filled the room, giving me my answer.

The answer neither of us would dare to say aloud.

"I'm going to get changed," I said and grabbed my pyjamas before heading into the bathroom.

When I came out, the light was already out and Natalie was tucked into her own bed, her back to me.

I turned out the bathroom light and headed to my bed, not saying anything as I got under my own covers and attempted to find sleep.

I FACED THE GROUP OF Slayers in front of me, my friends by my side as I raised my wand and flames wrapped around me.

But then, the Slayers were towering over me, and shackles shot up from the ground, trapping me in place.

I dropped my wand in shock, struggling against the shackles.

"There's no use, little Angelborn," the Slayer in front of me said before slamming his sword into Lena, piercing her heart.

"No!"

I continued to struggle as Charlotte joined her girlfriend on the floor.

"You can't save them," the Slayer said as he grabbed Natalie by the neck, ignoring her struggling as if it was nothing. "You dragged them into this, and they'll die for it."

He turned to Natalie. "The Vampire falls, after all."

At that, he brought his sword to Natalie's chest, before driving it into her.

I gasped as I awoke, turning desperately to see that Natalie was still asleep in her bed.

That she was fine and alive.

We'd never gone on the mission and the Slayers had never hurt her.

But that didn't mean that they wouldn't...

If she came with me in the morning, would she be okay?

Or would she 'fall'?

I climbed out of bed, grabbing my wand and casting a dampening spell to keep my steps silent and not risk waking Natalie.

If she caught me leaving, it would defeat the point.

I grabbed the armour Freya had given me and put it on as silently as possible, doubling up on dampening spells as Natalie remained still in her bed.

Once the armour was on, I gripped my wand tight and then shifted out.

Right to the edge of the wards surrounding the school, the frozen ground of the forest crunching beneath my feet.

I laid my wand flat in my palm before casting a locator spell.

The wand spun in my hand, eventually settling to point south.

I strode forward, my magic fuelling my muscles to make the walk shorter.

It didn't take me long to sense the first signs of magic.

The Council's listening post.

I used the sight Nature gave me to peer through the forest and identify the intruders.

There were only three men, two patrolling the perimeter and one inside a crude shack.

The inside of the shack glowed with magic, and I sifted through Maria's knowledge, realising that these were the spells being used to listen in on the school.

And if I disrupted the physical components – the runes and the focuses – I'd disrupt the spells.

And the outpost would be useless.

I cast a glamour, hiding myself from view as I continued to use Nature's sight to track the two patrolling Slayers.

Keeping out of their line of sight, even with my glamour, was almost trivial.

The shack didn't even have wards protecting it, so I slipped inside.

Leaving me with just one Slayer to deal with before destroying it.

The shack wasn't very big, allowing just enough room for me and the Slayer.

He wasn't facing me. His back was turned.

I gripped my wand and sifted through Maria's knowledge, looking for a spell I could use to disable him.

But her knowledge made it clear that the armour the Slayer was wearing was resistant to any and all magic.

Attempting to use magic to knock him out or send him away would only irritate him, and tell him that I was there.

Which would then lead to him alerting the others.

I wasn't even sure that I could take even one Slayer on in a fair fight, never mind more.

But where did that leave me?

Maria's knowledge gave me an answer, but I pushed it away.

He wasn't wearing a helmet. His throat was exposed, and a knife didn't need to use magic.

But that would mean killing someone.

That would mean killing someone that I wasn't actually in a fight with.

But... If I didn't, then he would likely kill me.

That didn't make it easier.

Before I could make a decision, the Slayer turned around.

My breath caught in my throat, hoping that my glamour held.

The Slayer glared within a moment, drawing his sword.

Shit.

I dodged out of the way of his strike, my mind reeling.

I didn't have a weapon.

I cast the spell to generate fire, speaking the incantation in my mind as I spun around to see the Slayer again.

I sent a spurt of fire hurtling towards him, but it hit his armour in a useless blast.

He didn't hesitate as he stormed forward with his weapon.

I dodged out of the way again, but lost my footing in the small space.

He kicked my legs out from underneath me, sending me hurtling towards one of the tables.

I crashed through the wood, splinters slicing open my cheek, moments before my jaw hit the ground with a thud that I felt all the way to the back of my skull.

The Slayer kicked me before I could scramble back to my feet, turning me enough to see that he had his sword raised, just above my eye.

And then he stopped.

A shadow moved swiftly across his neck, and the next thing I saw was a torrent of red as he collapsed to the ground, his throat slit.

I looked around the room, desperately searching for a sign of his attacker.

But there was no one there.

By the time I thought to look with Nature's sight, I was truly alone. Every Slayer was dead.

Then an almost blinding presence appeared, just outside the shack. "Amy?!"

I relaxed slightly at Freya's familiar voice, but I didn't have the strength to respond.

Pain radiated from my jaw and I feared moving it, my stomach dropping at the thought of just how bad the damage might be.

Thankfully, Freya opened the door to the shack without my answer, taking a moment to survey the room before her gaze fell on me and she rushed over.

"Amy!"

She was glowing with the same light that she'd used on Maureen in seconds, and the moment she touched me, the pain started to recede.

Shit, how bad had I looked that she had felt the need to use her healing magic so fast?

"Come on," Freya said once the pain had lessened enough that I didn't really fear moving my mouth. "Let's get you out of here."

She helped me to my feet and out of the shack.

Once we were to the door, she sent a blast of flames out behind us, reducing the shack to a crumbling pyre.

She led me to the edge of the forest, and as soon as we stepped through the trees, we entered Nature's clearing.

"Here," Freya said, navigating me to a rock to sit on. "Let me finish healing you."

I nodded, and it took all of my courage to risk opening my mouth to speak, still a little afraid of how bad I'd been hurt.

"How did you find me?" I asked, pain shooting through my jaw as I moved it, though nothing felt irreparably damaged and Freya's magic soon soothed the ache.

"Nature told me where you went. She didn't think that you could handle the fight on your own, and it looks like she was right. I'm assuming you didn't manage to slit that Slayer's throat while crumpled on the floor and unable to move your face."

I shook my head. "No, I didn't. He was going to kill me, and then... I don't know. I didn't see who did it. They stayed out of sight."

"Well, whoever they were, you likely owe them your life."

My stomach twisted at the truth of her words.

Freya sighed. "What were you thinking, Amy? Why did you go off on your own?"

I looked away. It seemed so foolish now that I was more than a few minutes away from the nightmare.

"I was worried that my friends would get hurt tomorrow. I... I had a nightmare where I saw them all die, and when I woke, I thought that if I handled the listening post on my own, I'd be able to keep them safe."

Freya shook her head. "I would be lying if I said that I hadn't thrown myself into almost suicidal danger to protect people before, but you know where that left me? With no friends and my marriage in shambles. Your friends knew the risk when they volunteered for this mission. How would you feel if one of them had gone off on their own tonight because they were worried about you getting hurt?"

I looked away, not wanting to admit that I'd be offended that they thought so little of my abilities. Or that they would have thought I'd want them to put themselves in danger for me.

But it was the truth.

"I'm sorry," I managed as tears welled in my eyes.

"It's okay," Freya said with a soft smile. "I think a near-death experience was lesson enough."

I nodded as the last of the pain from my fight finally dissipated, along with the glow around Freya.

"So," Freya said, "these nightmares. Was it just last night with the stress of the meeting, or were you having them before?"

"Before. Ever since Maria..." Freya thankfully nodded, indicating that I didn't need to continue. She knew what I meant. "I used to project myself into Maria's tower whenever I slept. And now I don't, and... I had a nightmare. About her dying. So, Natalie's been sleeping beside me to stave off the nightmares, and that was working, but... Well, it was probably going to be hard to keep it platonic if we kept doing it, given that we... We used to kind of have a thing. It never went anywhere because Natalie was afraid of biting me, but..."

"But being afraid of biting you doesn't mean that she doesn't like you? And that you don't like her?"

I nodded. "But then I fell in love with Willow, so it was all fine. But now Willow's not here, and I need someone, and... And it's complicated."

Freya frowned for a moment before shaking her head. "Sorry, I was wondering for a moment what the problem was. I forgot that not everyone is polyamorous."

I sighed. "Even if we all were, it's not as if I can talk to Willow about it. Wherever she is, my texts to her are being blocked."

Freya gave me a sympathetic look. "Yeah, that doesn't sound easy. But for when she does come back, you know that neither Vampires nor Elves tend to be monogamous, right? Drinking blood tends to be pretty intimate for a Vampire, and they can't drink from other Vampires, so they often have relationships both with other Vampires and their Human thralls. And Elves don't have nuclear family structures, they live pretty communally, so definitely knowing who's the father of your child, and therefore monogamy, was never a huge part of their society."

"Yeah, but Willow grew up with Witches."

"I know. I'm not saying that either of them would agree to anything like that, I'm just saying that you shouldn't rule it out until you can talk to Willow again. Though I appreciate that that doesn't solve your problem for now.

"Though, for tonight, why don't you stay here with me again? Maybe being so close to Nature will help."

I nodded, more than happy for the offer as my eyelids began to droop and exhaustion to set in.

Chapter Eight

I awoke with a groan, though any grogginess I felt swiftly melted away as I realised that I had woken up without nightmares.

Though, I was slightly stiff from having fallen asleep in the leather parts of my armour. I'd taken off the onyx plates to get comfortable, leaving myself in the black fabric beneath, but I'd left the leather on.

And no matter how soft the grass in Nature's clearing was, the stiff material had still caused me to develop several sore points in my joints as I had slept.

"Sleep okay?" Freya asked, already up.

I nodded.

"Maybe you should stay here at night," Freya said. "I'm sure Nature wouldn't mind, and maybe it would be good for you, even without me here."

I sighed. "Maybe..."

Freya gave me an understanding smile. "It's not the same as having Natalie beside you, is it?"

"No... But that's a problem in and of itself, isn't it? The fact that I feel this way about her at all..."

"Well then, maybe the space of staying here at night will be good for you."

I nodded once more before getting to my feet. "I guess I should head back before everyone wakes up and wonders where I am."

"Actually... They're probably already wondering. You've slept through your morning lessons. It's almost lunch."

I groaned at the news, glancing to the sky to see that the sun was, indeed, right above us.

Though I wasn't sure what time zone Nature's clearing was actually in. But it seemed to be night here when I came, so maybe it was just tailored to the time zone of the people to last enter.

"It's okay," Freya said. "I told Gail what happened as soon as you fell asleep. She's not happy that you went on your mission alone – neither is your aunt for that matter – but they'll understand that you needed the rest."

I groaned once more. "I get why you told Gail, but why did you have to tell my aunt as well? Were you trying to get me in trouble?"

Freya smirked. "No, she was with Gail."

I frowned. "Late at night?" It took another moment for me to put the pieces together. "Right, yeah, of course..."

Freya's smirk lessened. "Jess did mention that she's been trying to convince you to go home."

I pinched the bridge of my nose. "I'm not returning to the hell that is my parents' crumbling marriage. I just... I can't. I would rather fight a million Slayers."

Freya nodded in understanding as she made her way over and placed a hand on my shoulder. "I can't blame you for that. But if you do need a break, you could come to the Underworld for a bit."

"I... I don't know that I could. Not until we've dealt with the Council. Not until this is over."

"That could take years, Amy. Don't burn yourself out before you can finish this."

I sighed, and then nodded in resignation. "All right. If this goes on for too much longer... I'll think about it. But for now, I want to help deal with this trap the Council have set up for you."

"Do you promise not to go off on your own?"

"Yes, I promise."

"Okay. Then you should probably go and get dressed. If you get your friends and bring them to the infirmary, I'll tell Esme to meet us there."

I nodded before heading off, leaving Nature's clearing.

It led me out of the woods at the edge of the school, as close to the dormitories as possible.

I ran up to my room, taking the stairs two at a time, before hurrying in the shower and getting changed, not wanting to have to grab my friends from their afternoon classes once lunch ended.

As soon as I was dressed in my uniform, I headed for the dining hall, finding my friends at our usual table.

"Lia!" Lena cried as I approached, the first one to see me. "Where the hell have you been? Esme only told us that you were with Freya."

Natalie nodded as she turned to face me. "I woke up this morning and you were just gone. And you left your phone. Where were you?"

"I... I went to deal with the listening post myself."

Natalie's worried look turned to a frown. "You *what?*"

I sighed. "I was worried about Charlotte's prophecy, so I figured that it would be best if I could go alone, and none of you could be hurt."

Charlotte shook her head. "I never should have tried to look into the future."

"No, it's okay," I assured her quickly. "I shouldn't have let it get in my head, and I shouldn't have stormed off like I did."

Lena shrugged. "Well, at least you took care of the listening post, right? I mean, you shouldn't have gone alone, but if you managed it..."

I cringed. "I actually didn't manage it alone. One of the Slayers almost killed me. I don't know who stopped him, but... Someone did. And then Freya came to heal me and help me get away."

Natalie glared at me. "So you stormed off on your own last night and nearly got yourself killed? The prophecy spoke of you being in danger too, Amy."

"I know and I'm sorry. Trust me, I'm not in a hurry to go off on my own like that again.

"But, for now, Freya and Esme want to see us in the infirmary to talk about dealing with this trap the Council are setting up."

The others nodded and got up, following me as I headed to the infirmary.

I tried not to tense up, but it was difficult when I could still feel Natalie's glare.

I bit my lip. As I'd told Freya, I'd be angry if our positions were reversed, but I didn't know what to do with that.

So, I just kept moving towards the infirmary, focusing on the mission.

We arrived to see Esme, Sarah and Freya waiting for us.

"So," Esme said as we arrived, "with the listening post dealt with, I suppose we have our proof that the information was good. Which means moving on to stopping their trap before they can finish it."

I folded my arms. "Yeah, what exactly do we know about the trap?"

"They're building a prison. One that can hold a particularly strong magical being. My assumption would be that it's designed for Queen Freya."

"But wouldn't that start a war with the Underworld?"

Freya sighed, placing her hands on her hips. "I'm going to assume that they're going to frame me for something, and if they imprison me, not kill me... Well, Damon wouldn't risk starting a war unless he thought my life was in danger. They're more interested in proving that they're just as strong as me than actually fighting. If they imprison and humiliate me, it will get their point across."

Esme frowned. "And it will quiet any dissent within the Light beings, and allow the Council to continue their tyranny."

Freya gave a sardonic smile. "Nothing brings people together like beating up an enemy."

"So," I said, "how do we stop them?"

Esme smiled. "Well, we know where they're building this prison and we know that it's not finished. If we destroy it, we'll set their plans back by some time. Building a prison like this requires finding exactly the right place, where the magic will be perfectly attuned and that hasn't already been used over the centuries. I'm willing to bet that they've had this place held in reserve for decades, and if we take it from them, they'll have to go hunting for another.

"So, girls, if you all agree to come with me, we'll head out tomorrow morning. The Council will want to keep this place quiet, so I'm not expecting heavy guards. But if you don't feel you're ready, I can take Amazons."

Freya folded her arms. "That's almost as bad as me taking Demons. I doubt the Amazons want a war with the Council, either. Even you going isn't great, Esme."

"No, it's not, but while you can keep your distance, Queen Freya, I have to deal with the Council, and that means dismantling this prison before they can use it in my name, or the name of any other Light Witch."

Esme then turned to me and my friends. "But I am still reluctant to take children with me on a mission this dangerous. I really can find others to come with me."

Sarah placed her hand on Esme's shoulder, drawing her attention. "Esme, if they have control of a magical current, getting control back will take significant amounts of power. Power you would need from either an army or an Angel."

Esme sighed, turning to me. "Or an Angelborn. If you want to come, girls, it will just be the five of us. As I said, I do not think it will be heavily guarded, and we should be able to slip in and out without difficulty. But if you're not ready-"

"I'm ready," I said, without hesitation.

My mistake the night before had been going alone, but if I had my friends with me, we'd be fine.

Assuming they agreed to come.

"I'm ready too," Lena said, and Charlotte nodded.

Natalie hesitated and I bit my lip, wondering if she really would come with me.

But then she said, "I'm ready," and I let out a breath of relief.

Esme nodded. "Then meet me back here tomorrow morning after breakfast and we'll head out. If you need to spend time this afternoon preparing, I'll make sure you can be excused from classes."

"Thanks," I said before heading out of the infirmary, the others following.

I just headed back to the dormitories, almost on autopilot, though the others followed me, and Charlotte and Lena headed to their own room.

Leaving me and Natalie alone.

"So," I said as I closed our bedroom door behind us, "about last night..."

Natalie rounded on me with a glare. "It was stupid and reckless."

"I know."

"You could have been killed!"

"I know."

"Why the hell did you think it was a good idea?"

"Well, I'm kind of impulsive, if you haven't noticed. And it's worse when I haven't slept. I woke up from a nightmare where I watched all of you die on the mission. Where I watched *you* die. I couldn't let that happen. I know that it was dangerous, but protecting you seemed worth the danger."

Natalie sighed and I realised just how close we were standing as she softly said, "And what about you? Who was going to protect you?"

I reached out, once more losing the fight with my impulsiveness as I placed a hand on her arm.

She looked up, her gaze locking with mine as my breath caught in my throat.

Natalie parted her lips slightly and I saw the white of her fangs. A thrill of excitement went through me at the sight, manifesting in a small current of Energy.

That was enough for Natalie to pull away, her fingers going to her lips as she retracted the fangs.

She groaned once they were gone, running her hand through her hair. "This isn't fair. How can I feel something this strong without a drop of blood in my system?"

I knew what she meant because I'd been asking myself the same thing. Only, instead of 'without blood' it was 'when I was still in love with someone else'.

And I was. Willow's absence was an open wound in my heart, producing an ache so strong that I was only dealing with it by letting myself forget. By just leaning into the lack of object permanence that came with ADHD, making it difficult to conceptualise that she was truly gone.

But I wanted her back. More than anything, if I had a single wish, it would be to see her again.

So, how could I feel like this for Natalie?

Probably the same way Freya loved both her husband and her heartbond. And how Damon loved both Freya and Mr Stiles.

Natalie shook her head. "I'm not supposed to feel like this."

That pulled me from my thoughts, and I closed the space between us once more. "Maybe we shouldn't focus so much on what we 'should' feel. Trust me, as someone who doesn't always feel things the 'correct' way, it's an easy path to despair."

"So, what? I'm just supposed to accept the fact that I'm in love with someone who loves someone else? That every second we're together, my heart breaks with the knowledge that she will never be mine? That every time I picture my future, I can't imagine it without her beside me?"

I shrugged. "Why not? Who do you think is judging you? Me? What room do I have to judge when I feel the same way about you. And I also feel that way about Willow. And every moment I'm not scared for my life or grieving Maria, I'm trying to reconcile those two things.

"But the idea of having multiple relationships is new to me, so that's why I'm struggling. Isn't that normal for Vampires? Don't you often have relationships with other Vampires and with Human thralls? You've mentioned that your parents have thralls…"

"They do," Natalie said. "They love their thralls as much as they love each other, and their thralls also raised me. But you're neither Human nor a Vampire, so I wasn't thinking of things in those terms."

"Well, why not? If it's possible there, why not here?"

Natalie sighed as she folded her arms before dropping her gaze. "Look, Amy, there's no point in talking about this now. We can't be together because even if we agree, Willow might not. I'm not going to entertain the possibility of us being together when it might be all ripped away the moment Willow returns. That… That's more than I can take."

I nodded, understanding her worry all too well.

And knowing that nothing I said would change things.

I HEADED TO THE FOREST as it got late, and the moment I stepped through the trees, I entered Nature's clearing.

Nature herself was already there, in her wolf form, and came over to greet me.

I smiled, glad that I wasn't alone as I settled down to sleep, Nature settling beside me, warding off the nightmares.

Chapter Nine

I awoke with a groan, though I soon smiled as I realised that I hadn't had any nightmares.

No, Nature had kept them at bay.

I kept smiling as I stroked her furry ears and she stirred slightly.

"Thank you," I said before checking my phone and realising that it was nearly breakfast. And I needed a shower after sleeping in the woods.

I stood up and left the clearing before shifting back to my room.

Natalie was already awake and fully dressed in the same combat dress she'd worn to Maria's funeral, her long, ebony hair tied back in a tight French plait.

"Amy," she said as I arrived. "Sleep well?"

There was tension in her tone and, perhaps, a little guilt.

My stomach twisted. It wasn't her fault that things had gotten so complicated between us.

That she couldn't chase away my nightmares anymore.

I forced myself to smile, determined to make things as normal they could possibly be between us.

Not that I even knew what that meant anymore...

"Yeah, staying in Nature's clearing was great. I slept right through the night." I forced my smile to widen, hoping that she wouldn't worry.

It wasn't sure if I was thankful or not that she smiled in return, clearly relieved that we didn't have to go back to either sharing a bed or my nightmares returning.

As if the way we had been spending the last few nights had been some great pain for her.

But it had been, that was the frustrating part. I wanted to be annoyed, I wanted to be offended, but I knew just how painful it had been for her.

And, in all honesty, how painful it had been for me when I wasn't ignoring how I felt about her.

"I guess I had better hurry and get dressed," I said as I headed over to the wardrobe where I had stashed the armour Freya had given me.

Once I had it on, Natalie and I made our way down to the infirmary, where everyone is waiting for us.

Everyone, including Ms Griffin and Auntie Jess.

Neither of them looked happy. Ms Griffin had her hands on her hips and was wearing a slight frown, and Auntie Jess had her arms folded.

Both of them were aiming their unhappy looks equally between Esme and Freya.

As I entered the room, Auntie Jess made her way over to me. "Amy, I know that you said that you wanted to help with this mission, but you know you don't have to go, right? This doesn't have to be your responsibility."

"The Council made it my responsibility when they killed Maria. I'm not going to walk away from that."

Auntie Jess shook her head. "You're still just a student, Amy. There are other people – more experienced people – who can do this."

"No, there aren't." I turned to Freya, sure that my auntie wouldn't listen to me.

Freya sighed. "I told you this before, Jessica. The only power strong enough to stop the Council's prison from being constructed is an Angel. But my powers mean that I can't risk getting into a fight on Earth."

"Then send an army instead, enough Witches-"

Esme stepped forward, giving my auntie an apologetic look. "Enough Witches would mean declaring war on the Council. I don't think any of us are ready for that."

"And what if Amy's not ready for this mission?"

"I am!" I said, stepping forward. "I can do this. If this is what it takes to take down the Council, then I can do it. I swear."

Auntie Jess didn't exactly seem convinced, but Ms Griffin placed a hand on her shoulder.

"I don't like it either," Ms Griffin said. "But Freya and Esme are right. Amy is likely the only one powerful enough to do this without starting a war. And she won't be safe if that happens either."

Auntie Jess sighed, pinching the bridge of her nose for a long moment before nodding. "Okay," she said before shifting several vials into her hands, a combination of silver and purple.

There were four purple vials, and she divided them between me, Natalie, Charlotte and Lena.

"These potions will enhance your strength, stamina and reflexes, and they should work to help you heal faster if you get injured. They won't be able to stop anything fatal, but they should help. If you drink them now, they should kick in quickly." She then handed each of us four small vials of the silver potions as we knocked back the purple. "These healing potions should keep you up and running, even if something else were to happen to you. I decanted them into smaller vials, so they will be easier for you to use just a small amount as and when you need it."

"Thank you," I said as I placed the healing vials on my belt for easy access. As soon as I was sure they were secure, I rushed forward and hugged my auntie tight around the waist.

"Really," I mumbled into her shirt. "Thank you."

She sighed, a small amount of the tension she had been carrying trickling away. "Just... Be careful, okay? I can't lose you, Amy."

"You won't," I promised as I pulled away.

Realising that we were done, Esme stepped forward. "Well, if you're all ready, I will activate the portal that will take us to the Council's base of operations." She nodded to a portal she'd already drawn on the wall before she turned to Auntie Jess and Ms Griffin. "I'll take care of them. I promise."

"You'd better," Auntie Jess said, her previous glare returning and leaving no uncertainty that returning all of us home safely was in Esme's best interests.

Esme just nodded before turning to me and my friends.

"Ready?" she asked, and I had to admit that I was getting sick of the question.

But still, I nodded.

"Then let's go."

She took a vial of glittering powder and threw the contents over the chalk, causing it to light up.

Once the light had formed the portal, Esme strode through, hesitating for only a moment to make sure that we were following.

We stepped through after her, arriving in a large, stone room. The walls curved over us, forming a domed roof above, and intricate runes were carved into the stone. But before I had a chance to examine them closely, they began to glow red.

"Lena!" Esme yelled. "Those walls are about to crack and let through enough water to drown us all."

"On it!"

The walls began to crack above us and water began to seep through, but only for a moment before Lena raised her hands, holding it in place with her powers.

"I don't know how long I can hold it," Lena groaned through gritted teeth.

Charlotte then took out her wand, silently casting a spell that reached out with a net of glowing white magic, creeping over the cracked wall and holding it in place.

Lena dropped her arms with a gasp, resting them on her knees as she leaned forward, gulping down air.

She turned to Esme as she finally caught her breath. "That wasn't a small amount of water. Where are we, the sea bed?"

"Yes, though I had not thought that they would risk flooding their own facility to prevent intruders."

Charlotte eyed her spell warily. "I'm not sure how long we've got until this breaks."

"Can you cast it again if it does?"

"If Lena holds the water back while I do, then yes."

"Then the two of you should stay here while the rest of us move on."

I frowned. "Are we sure we want to split up? What if we get caught? Won't it be harder to fight?"

"It might be, but we cannot fight every Slayer here and if this room floods, they will be alerted to our presence, and we will be trapped in here with them. As Lena said, we are underwater and this room is the only one that portals can be used in."

Lena gave me a slightly cocky smile. "Don't worry, Lia. We've got this. And if the Slayers get in here, I've got more than enough water to take care of them."

I nodded and turned to Esme. "So, what's the plan from here?"

"We sneak through the facility, find the heart of the imprisoning spell they're casting and destroy it. Once that's done, we should have control of the current of magic here, and that will allow us to deal with the Slayers and take control of this place for ourselves, taking it out of the Council's hands."

I nodded as Esme headed to the only door out of the room.

As we neared it, I grabbed my wand and almost instinctively cast a glamour over myself, Esme and Natalie.

As we disappeared, I switched to looking through Nature's sight. I might be good with glamours, but even I couldn't fool that.

Esme looked down at her hands. "I'm assuming this is your doing, Amelia?"

"Yeah."

"It's a good glamour, but remind me to show you how to cast one that allows your allies to see you when we get back. It's not always as foolproof as other glamours, but trying to tell your allies where you are can be just as dangerous as a weaker glamour."

"Well, I can see where you are using Nature's sight, and you know where we're supposed to be going, so I can follow you and lead Natalie."

Natalie frowned. "How will you lead me when you can't see me?"

I reached out and took her hand in answer, only realising what I'd done beyond practicality as my skin tingled where I touched hers.

Still, she didn't let go. She just looked down at our hands before saying, "Yeah, I guess that works," her voice barely more than a whisper.

"Well, if you're ready," Esme said, her no-nonsense tone cutting across the tension and reminding us exactly where we were, "we should head through. Stay close to me – I should be able to sense the centre of the magic – and even with the glamour, try to keep to the shadows."

I nodded, before remembering that she couldn't see.

"Understood," I said aloud and Esme then turned to the door, finally opening it to reveal a stone corridor, with glowing blue stones littered through the walls to illuminate the way with an almost eerie light.

I followed Esme, trying to keep my attention both on her and on keeping Natalie close, though I did occasionally scan the area to see if any Slayers were approaching.

Some got close, but every time they did, Esme steered us away.

Even if they might have seen past the glamour, they didn't get the chance before I started to see the threads of magic around us getting brighter through Nature's sight.

We headed towards the brightness until it was so overwhelming that I worried about not seeing Slayers through it.

I strained my sight, seeing two Slayers ahead as we rounded a corner.

But before I had a chance to respond, Esme pulled a vial from her side and launched it at the ground between the Slayers.

The glass smashed on the ground and dark grey smoke leaked from the bottle.

The Slayers both jumped at the sound of the glass smashing, but the smoke reached them before they could do anything, and they both collapsed down to the ground, unconscious.

Leaving the door to the glowing light completely unguarded.

I sighed with relief at how easily the guards had gone down.

And that Esme had been the one to deal with them.

My mind drifted back to the listening outpost, and the Slayer I'd had the opportunity to kill.

Before I'd let the chance slip away from me, unable to do what had to be done.

I clenched my fists, frustrated at both the memory and also the knowledge that even going through that near-death experience probably hadn't made me any more likely to raise a blade to the throat of an unsuspecting opponent.

But then, what did I expect? If I couldn't even stomach the thought of animals being slaughtered for my dinner, why did I think that I could fight someone to the death?

But it wasn't that I thought I could, it's that I'd thought I wouldn't have to.

The thought of having to hadn't even occurred to me.

And I'd almost ended up dead.

Even with that harsh lesson, I was still cowering behind others, letting them do my work for me.

Maybe I wasn't as ready for this as I'd thought...

I pushed that thought aside. Yes, Esme had dealt with the guards, but while they were unconscious, their chests were still slowly moving up and down, indicating that the potion hadn't killed them.

I just needed to give myself options, like Esme had with the potion. That was all.

I took a deep breath and refocused as Esme headed for the door.

She turned to me – or my general direction, given that she couldn't actually see me – before she opened it. "Can you sense anyone beyond?"

I peered through the door. It was difficult to see, the magic in the room was so bright, but I couldn't see anything that looked like a person.

"No," I said. "The room looks empty."

Esme nodded before finally opening the door with one hand, her other tightly gripping her wand.

I switched back to my regular sight, as Nature's sight was so overwhelmed by the magic of the room.

Esme opened the door to reveal a large, stone chamber, in the centre of which was a stone pillar, covered in intricately carved runes, though they weren't finished.

"Is that the imprisoning spell?" I asked.

"Yes," Esme said as she made her way over to it. "Thankfully, it looks like we got here before they completed it. Though, I'm going to need to see my hands to start dismantling it. Then you'll need to strike the final blow, Amelia."

I nodded, dropping the glamour.

As soon as I did, the door closed behind us.

Esme turned at the sound, but as she did, a figure shifted in behind her.

And Esme collapsed forward.

A knife in her back.

"No!" I yelled, going to grab one of the healing potions at my side, but someone grabbed my arms from behind, keeping me in place.

"Now, now," the figure behind Esme said, drawing my attention to her as I realised that it was Dana, "it's too late for that."

Dark Energy crackled over my skin in fury, but then Dana moved over to me, grabbing my wand before I could let any of it loose.

And she snapped it in half.

My Energy immediately cascaded out, every ounce of my magical strength fuelled into a blast that I couldn't focus without my wand.

Dana's armour easily absorbed it.

I gasped for air, the blast having taken everything from me.

I'd never given thought as to what would happen if I lost my wand, but I knew now as I tried desperately to grasp the last of my magical reserves, and found that they refused to answer me, slipping through my grasp like smoke.

Dana then moved over to Natalie, who had a Slayer keeping her tight in his grasp.

Dana took her wand with ease, though my attention was swiftly drawn to the blood slowly seeping through Natalie's dress, surrounding a nasty wound in her side.

I winced. Of course they'd injured her. I might be useless without a wand, but Natalie had Vampiric strength.

Strength she couldn't access when so badly hurt if the sheen of sweat coating her sickly pale skin was any indication.

Given how pale she was to start, the fact that she now looked so much worse made my stomach churn.

That churn turned into a lurch as Dana snapped Natalie's wand and Natalie jerked forward, only to stumble, the Slayer holding her having to keep her upright.

Dana then grabbed the healing potions on Natalie's belt and dropped them to the ground before smashing them beneath her heel.

She turned to the Slayer holding me. "Make sure she has no potions on her either, and then lock them in one of the cells. Don't kill them, I don't want an incident."

The Slayer holding Natalie frowned. "This one's not gonna last."

"If she bleeds out, she bleeds out, just don't finish the job yourself. That will be harder to explain away."

She then looked down at Esme with a smile. "Once you're done with the girls, prepare to pack up. It looks like our work here is done for now."

I followed her gaze, and switched to Nature's sight.

My relief at that portion of my magic still working was short-lived, however, as I followed Dana's gaze and saw that there was no life left in Esme.

Just an empty corpse.

I shuddered, looking over to see if Natalie was okay.

Ice ran down my back as I saw that her life force was faint and indistinct.

And swiftly fading.

If I didn't get her to a healer soon...

I tried not to think about it, knowing that giving into despair was the last thing that would help here.

I had to focus if I wanted to get us out of here.

The Slayers dragged us through a couple of corridors before reaching a small, stone cell and throwing us inside.

The one holding me threw me hard enough that I crashed to the ground, barely saving my face from hitting the stone, but only by sacrificing a good chunk of the skin on my hands, blood seeping over my palms as the door closed behind me.

I gave the door one quick look to see that it was locked with magic that I couldn't get past without my wand before focusing all of my attention on Natalie.

She was slumped in the corner, her hands tightly gripping her wound.

"Nat," I breathed as I kneeled down beside her. "Shit, that looks..."

"I'm fine," she grunted, cutting me off. "I'll be fine."

I sighed, not believing her for a moment. I reached down to my belt, only to find it empty.

Right, Dana had told the Slayer holding me to take my healing potions.

Which meant that I had nothing to heal Natalie with.

I had no potions and no wand to cast a healing spell...

A stray strand of dark hair fell in her eyes and I instinctively reached out to brush it away.

She stiffened and I momentarily worried that I had hurt her.

Before I saw the red of my palms.

"Blood," I said, thinking aloud before turning to Natalie. "Would blood help to heal you?"

Natalie groaned, looking away.

Her silence was answer enough.

"Nat, you have to drink from me. You... You're not doing great, and I can't get us out of here. Even if Lena and Charlotte realise something's wrong and come to get us... I don't think we have that kind of time.

"I'm useless without my wand, but if you get your strength back, you'll be able to get both of us out of here. It's our only shot."

Natalie shook her head, though even that small movement caused her to wince.

She took a deep, steadying breath before speaking once more. "No, Amy, I can't. If I bite you – if I drink your blood – it will bind us together. Permanently."

I stared at her incredulously. "Natalie, if you don't do it, you'll die. Being bound together is a small price to pay for your life."

Natalie still didn't meet my gaze.

"Please, Nat, I would rather have you bonded to me and alive, than be unbonded and lose you." I took her hand and held it tight. "I really can't lose you, Nat."

She still didn't look convinced, but what little strength she had crackled into a small wave of Dark Energy as pain radiated from the wound and her skin got even colder against mine.

She was running out of time.

She must have realised it as well as she finally met my gaze, apology and despair held in equal measure as she said, "I'm sorry."

She was on me faster than I could track, and I barely had time to register the feel of her body against mine before her fangs sank into the soft skin of my neck.

It should have hurt.

I knew, intellectually, that it should have hurt. That I should be horrified or frightened by the feel of my blood pouring into her mouth.

But I couldn't feel anything over the waves of ecstasy radiating out from the wound, every nerve-ending in my body turned up to eleven as I became hyper aware of Natalie's body pressed against mine, every ounce of feeling for her I'd buried deep to survive her rejection rushing through me at full force.

I never wanted her to stop.

And then I started to feel something else.

Her magic flowing into mine like a soothing river, making its way lazily through me. Her magic entwined with mine as it went until I was no longer sure what where I ended and she began.

My heart melted at the need to hold her close and never let her go.

My Natalie.

My love.

The thought was crystal clear in its truth as our magic bound us together, giving form to our feelings.

I barely registered that I was starting to feel light-headed, but Natalie pulled away as soon as the thought came to me, and I felt a wave of worry from her, as clearly as I had ever felt anything.

I could *feel* her.

Before that moment, I hadn't been feeling anything from her, but I swiftly realised that that was because there had been no difference in our feelings.

The ecstasy, the need for her, and the rightness of the bond had all been mirrored in her feelings perfectly.

She leaned forward to gently lick my bite-marks, the move stopping the blood now pouring down my neck.

She took a moment to lick up that too, but I didn't mind. If I was going to lose blood, it might as well not go to waste.

And I couldn't deny that the feel of her tongue moving gently against my skin-

"We need to focus," Natalie said, yanking me from my thoughts as she pulled away.

"Right, yes," I managed. We were still in a prison, I reminded myself.

"How do you feel?" I asked, though the question was redundant.

I knew exactly how she felt through the bond, my blood having closed her wound and strengthened her beyond even what she normally felt.

"I'm fine now," she said as she looked me over. "And Amy... Thank you. Really. If you hadn't-"

"I couldn't lose you," I told her firmly. "No matter what."

She just nodded before standing up and making her way over to the door.

"Are you ready?" she asked.

"Yeah," I said as I forced myself to my feet. I had to grip the wall as the room spun around me, but I managed it.

I might be a little light-headed, but we didn't have time for that. We needed to get to the others to make sure that they were okay.

Natalie then struck the door, and it flew from its hinges in one smooth motion, collapsing to the floor of the corridor.

"Where should we go?" Natalie asked. "I mean, we still haven't taken down the facility, and Esme..."

I could feel her guilt and fury through the bond, her need for revenge mirroring my own.

It was strange, to be able to feel everything she felt, though not as invasive or unnerving as I might have thought.

But I could also feel the effect my blood was having on her. The way it was amplifying her feelings far beyond what she usually dealt with.

Despite what I could feel through the bond, my own needs to prove myself by completing the mission and get revenge for Esme were tempered by my exhaustion, and the fact that the damn corridor just wouldn't stop spinning.

Natalie made her way over, her worry unusually present on her face.

Just when I no longer needed her facial expressions to tell me how she was feeling...

"I need to get you home," Natalie said, any other focus melting away to allow tender worry to take its place.

I couldn't help but melt into her arms as she wrapped them around me.

"It's okay," she said. "I've got you."

Of course she did. She was my bonded.

I hadn't even really thought about what that meant for magical beings before, but now I was sure.

It was etched into my magic along with the part of Natalie's now entwined with mine.

"Come on," Natalie said. "Let's get to Lena and Charlotte."

I nodded as Natalie led me down the corridors, back the way we'd come.

I considered looking through Nature's sight, to see if there were any Slayers in our path, but before I could, one rounded the corner, right in front of us.

Natalie moved me aside, standing between me and the Slayer, just as he turned to face us.

Michael.

My breath caught in my throat as he drew his weapon.

Natalie didn't have a weapon.

And neither did I.

Hell, I probably couldn't even move from where I was standing without falling over.

Natalie kicked him square in the chest before he could bring his sword down, knocking him back.

He stumbled, and she moved faster than I could see, striking him again.

As she went for a third blow, however, his own speed picked up, and while he didn't get her with his blade, he hit her hard enough to send her stumbling into the wall.

"No, Nat!" I cried, and Michael whipped his head around to face me.

He grinned as soon as he saw me, barely managing to stand as I leaned heavily against the wall.

He stalked forward, and I readied myself as best I could, knowing that my only option would likely be to dive out of his way and hope that Natalie got to him before he went for a second blow.

I readied my muscles as I watched his sword, waiting for the exact timing I needed to get away.

But his blow never came.

I dared take my eyes from the weapon to see why he hadn't struck, only to see a torrent of red cascading down his armour.

His throat was slit.

Who had slit his throat?

Natalie didn't have a weapon.

Michael dropped to his knees, and then completely to the ground, revealing the figure behind him.

She was in black armour that was thinner than my own and completely matte, seeming to draw in light, and her long red hair was tied back in an intricate style that kept it on her head and out of the way, but I would recognise her freckled visage anywhere.

"Willow."

She gave me a small smile. "Hey." She then looked me over and frowned, presumably as she saw how heavily I was leaning on the wall.

"Shit, you're hurt."

She sheathed her blood soaked *Fin'Hathan* blade as she hurried over to me, placing her hand on my cheek as she looked me over, presumably for any sign of injury.

She stopped still as she spotted the bite marks on my neck.

"A Vampire bite..." She turned to Natalie, who was finally making her way over from where Michael had knocked her down, her new scrapes healing rapidly.

Natalie cringed under Willow's gaze, though the tension in Willow's frame melted away as she saw the hole in Natalie's dress, the remnants of her wound still pink beneath, and her dress soaked in blood.

"Shit, Natalie," Willow said as she failed to tear her gaze from her wound. "They almost killed you... I am so sorry. I didn't think your wound was that bad, and... And the Slayers taking you away meant that Dana was alone."

I frowned. "Wait, you were there?"

She nodded as she turned back to me. "Yes. I'm sorry. I came here to stop Dana and Michael, but... I couldn't stop them from killing Esme. By the time I'd realised what they'd done..."

"It's okay," I said, knowing that none of us could have moved fast enough to stop her. "You did what you could."

"But if I'd followed you two instead of staying behind to deal with Dana..."

"What's done is done," I said. "I'm just glad that you're here now."

Willow gave me a small smile before leaning forward, her lips meeting mine in a clash of longing that her Energy told me we'd both been doing our best to ignore ever since the Council had had her expelled.

The bite marks on my neck ached, reminding me that our reunion wasn't nearly as simple as I had hoped every time I'd thought of it.

Willow pulled away with a sigh that said that her thoughts were in exactly the same place.

But rather than acknowledging the Vampire in the room, she instead turned to face both me and Natalie as best as she could when we were standing so far apart.

"My mission was to deal with Michael and Dana and poison the magical currents here so that they couldn't be harnessed for the next hundred years. Michael and Dana are now dealt with, but the magical currents..."

I groaned, realising the problem. "You need an Angel to reclaim them. Or at least an Angelborn."

"Well, I'm definitely not strong enough. I guess that's why Esme brought you with her."

I nodded, not finding the strength to do anything more.

Natalie stepped forward. "Willow, she's not strong enough. She can barely stand."

Willow frowned. "What did they do to her?"

Natalie cringed. "This wasn't them. They did break her wand, but most of it... It's me. I needed so much blood to heal, and by the time I realised what I'd done..."

Willow's frown deepened. "And she's still this bad? Even after you enthralled her?"

"I... I didn't. It all happened so fast..."

"Natalie, enthrallment helps with healing. If your Vampire magic has been replenished by her blood, then it's the least you can do. Isn't that the point of enthrallment? To repay the thrall for their sacrifice."

"Yes, but Amy's not my thrall! And it... Willow, you know how it will make her feel."

"And if you don't do it, we lose this mission." Willow turned to me. "Would you rather Natalie got you well enough to finish this mission, or do you want to limp home and have Esme die for nothing?"

"Finish the mission. Of course I want to finish the mission and have Esme's death mean something."

Natalie frowned as she stepped closer. "Amy... Enthrallment can be just as intense as the bite. Even if I use it on you, there's no guarantee that you'll be strong enough to complete the mission. It can't work miracles."

"But if there's a chance... I can't let this prison stand, Natalie. Not if I can stop it. And I don't see how we can end up any deeper in this than we already are."

Natalie frowned as her gaze drifted to the bite marks on my neck.

"All right," she said after a moment before stepping forward, her hand going to my cheek as she met my gaze.

Her crimson eyes seemed to almost glow for a moment, and I found myself unable to look away as I melted under her touch.

I felt as if I'd stepped into a hot bath, the water replenishing every physical ache I had, and soothing all of my anxiety over the nearly failed mission.

Natalie's hand went to my waist, keeping me steady, and something else started to follow the soothing feeling.

A slow burning fire, directed entirely at my bonded.

The next thing I knew, I'd closed the space between us, kissing her slow and deep as I sent my feelings through the bond, showing her exactly how much I needed to be out of there.

How much I needed to be with her, the two of us alone and able to explore our bond in every possible way.

Natalie closed her eyes, reciprocating the kiss for a moment.

But the break in eye contact broke the spell and I suddenly remembered where we were.

And who was watching us.

Natalie responded to my feelings before I could, jumping away from me.

"Amy, I... I'm sorry. I tried to warn you, but... I still shouldn't have..."

Before I could figure out what to say, Willow turned to me. "How do you feel?" she asked.

As if she hadn't just watched me making out with someone else.

"Better," I managed, unable to really think of an answer beyond that simple truth.

"Enough to take control of the magical currents?"

"I think so."

She nodded. "Then we'd better get moving."

"Willow," I said, stopping her before she could storm off. "What just happened... The enthrallment..."

"I know," she said, her voice soft. "For now, we should focus on the mission."

"Right. The mission." I followed her as she headed back towards the centre of the magical currents. Towards the room where Esme had died... "That would be the mission that we both seem to be trying to accomplish. The mission that you seem to be doing much better at."

Willow gave a sheepish shrug. "They weren't expecting me. The *Fin'Hathan* weren't involved in this until I convinced them, and even then... This is my mission. My final trial." Her features then turned grim as she tightened her jaw. "As for you... They were very much expecting you. This whole thing... They did intend for this prison to maybe hold Queen Freya – or you, Amelia – one day, but they leaked the details of their plan to Esme knowing that she would come here. Your mission was over the moment her magical signature entered the central room, no matter how many glamours you had her under."

"This... This whole trap was for *Esme*?"

Willow nodded. "Dana wants control of the Amazons back. And Michael wants her to have it, given that she's an ally to him and the Council. I'm sorry, Amelia. I should have done a better job of protecting her. I was so focused on following Dana, I didn't realise you were here until it was too late." She then cringed as she glanced at the remnant of Natalie's wound once more. "And if I hadn't been so focused on completing the mission..."

"If you hadn't been so focused, we would still have to deal with Dana and Michael. They probably wouldn't so easily let us just take this place."

"Well, no, I suppose not."

At that, we arrived at our destination.

"Do you know what to do?" Willow asked as I approached the stone pillar in the centre of the room.

The runes had clearly been altered and I turned to Willow with a frown.

"I tried to dismantle it," she explained. "But when I finally tried to take it down, I wasn't strong enough."

I nodded, realising that Willow had gotten the spell to the same point Esme was going to get it to, before I took it down for good.

My stomach twinged at the reminder of Esme, and I couldn't help but glance at the floor.

To see the pool of blood where she had once been.

Where she was now...

I tried to push that thought away, not sure I wanted to know the answer.

I focused on the spell in front of me, reaching out with my magic to connect to it.

Thankfully, Willow had reduced it down to raw magic.

Something I didn't need my wand to connect to.

As soon as I connected to the magic, I recognised Dana's signature, and fury filled me.

All I could see was her knife in Esme's back as I grabbed her magic, overwhelming it with my own.

I fuelled everything into grabbing her magic, taking out every bit of rage within me on what little remained of Dana now that Willow had taken care of the rest.

I tore the magic from the currents, freeing them from Dana's influence, and the last of Dana's magic dissipated from the world.

I stumbled forward, the world spinning around me.

"Amy!"

Cold hands grabbed me, stopping me from hitting the ground, as the world went dark.

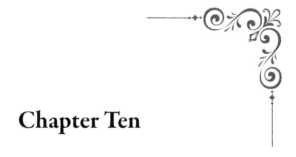

Chapter Ten

I groaned as I awoke, every cell of my body on fire.

"Amy," I heard Freya's familiar voice say, her relief more than clear.

I did my best to force my eyes open, but I didn't have the strength.

Slowly, despite my eyes remaining closed, I became aware of a soft white light washing over me, easing my pain.

Freya took my hand and I could feel the magic washing over me more strongly.

Freya's healing magic.

I finally managed to get my eyes open, seeing that Freya was sitting next to me on the bed, the light surrounding her as well, going out behind her to form a large pair of white wings.

"Amy," she said with a relieved smile as she saw that I was awake, though it was quickly replaced by a frown. "That was too close, Amy. If you'd gotten back here even a moment later..."

I barely managed to nod, more than aware of that issue when everything hurt like hell.

I hadn't felt this bad since...

My old scars throbbed in reminder.

Yeah, I knew what almost dying felt like, and this...

I had fuelled all of my magic into stopping those magical currents, and it had taken nearly everything I had.

Auntie Jess approached, giving me a relieved smile as she saw that I was awake.

"Hey," she said. "Willow said that you were already wiped out when you went to destroy the prison spell. Amy... You should have just let it go."

"No..." I managed, my throat feeling like I'd been gargling broken glass. "I couldn't... Couldn't have let Esme die for nothing..."

Auntie Jess winced before sighing. "I assumed when she didn't come back with you, but..."

A chill went down my spine as I realised that no one had told her what had happened to Esme.

I guess I hadn't been out as long as I thought.

I looked over to the other side of the room and saw that the others were standing there, explaining everything to Sarah.

Well, Natalie and Willow were standing. Lena looked exhausted, and Charlotte was sitting next to her on one of the infirmary beds.

I guess keeping our escape dry had taken a toll...

Never mind me, if we'd delayed for a moment later, would we have been able to leave at all?

Auntie Jess drew my attention back with a sigh as her hand went to my neck.

To the bite marks there.

"I'm guessing Natalie had to take a lot from you to heal, given the size of her wound and the amount of blood she appears to have lost."

I just stared at my auntie as she moved her hand from my neck and I realised how obvious what had happened must be.

I moved my hand to the bite marks.

How obvious were they?

For the first time since having it done, I almost regretted cutting my hair so short, leaving the marks completely exposed.

"Did you lose the healing potions?" Auntie Jess asked.

I nodded before turning my attention back to the others.

From the somber looks on Natalie and Willow's faces, it was clear that they were still explaining what had happened to Sarah.

And it was more than clear when Sarah balled her hands into fists, Dark Energy crackling across them.

"Shit," Freya muttered before leaving my side, the loss of her healing magic leaving me cold as she headed over to her friend.

Though I couldn't blame her for going.

Not if the others had just told her what had happened to Esme.

"Damn it," Sarah said, loud enough for me to hear now that I was paying attention. "Creator damn it, I told her not to trust Dana's old people. And now with her gone... Shit. They're going to try to take the Amazons back, and Esme didn't have enough time to put infrastructure in place to slow them down if they did. Not while she was so busy trying to appease them."

Freya placed her hand on Sarah's shoulder. "It's okay," she said and signed with one hand. "I'll help you stop them, Sarah. In whatever way I can."

"Except you can't, Freya. This isn't the Underworld where you can fight your political opponents into submission. They will declare me unfit to take Esme's place – many thought me too young to be her deputy, and I am certainly too young to replace her – so they will hold another election and we barely won the last one by the skin of our teeth. The older Witches will turn out in droves to stop a repeat of the last election, and what do you think will happen to Esme's supporters with her gone? There is no clear replacement for Esme besides me, and I'm too young to run in the election. Without a good replacement, we'll lose support, and we'll lose a hell of a lot more to people losing hope. Young Witches worked themselves to the bone to get Esme elected, and Dana killed her for it. How am I supposed to convince them that showing up a second time is worth it?"

Freya hesitated for a moment before sighing. "Maybe you don't. Maybe you convince them to actually stand up to Dana. If Dana's willing to kill-"

"I will not stoop to her level."

"I'm not saying that you start murdering people. I'm just saying that maybe fighting isn't the worst way to approach this."

Willow stepped forward. "Regardless of whether or not you're willing to fight, rooting out the corruption in the Amazons is my mission now. I'll do it alone if I have to, but I would rather have help."

Sarah shook her head. "You can't just go around assassinating everyone who worked with Dana."

"Why not? They all have blood on their hands, and not just Esme's. How many Witches have they abandoned over the years? Themiscyra was supposed to be a safe haven. Do you know how many Witches have died because they were denied that? I do. When I looked into it for the *Fin'Hathan*, I hoped that I would find that I was wrong. That the way the Amazons and the Council had treated me and Amy was just a coincidence, not a sign of larger corruption. What I found instead is that the Amazons have turned their back on us. Creator, did you know that they could have made Themiscyra a safe place during the last Alternate Timeline? That they had more than enough room to give shelter during the War to everyone. Esme had a plan, and argued for it with everything she had. But they prioritised Amazons, and pure-blooded Witches after that.

"The Amazons have been ruled by the same three families of pure-blooded Witches for centuries, and each and every one was committed to using their power to keep it that way - to keep their little club of Witches as exclusive as possible - no matter how much it hurt other Witches. Esme was the first break in that, and they killed her for it.

"They have shown that they're not going to play fair, and if we keep trying to, we're going to lose."

Sarah sighed, taking several moments before saying, "There has to be another way."

"If you find one, let me know. But until you do, I have a mission to complete."

Auntie Jess sighed as she turned to me. "I guess there's no way to convince you not to follow Willow into this, is there?"

"No, there isn't," I managed, my throat still raw and my voice still rasping.

"Okay. But... If she tries to barrel into this, try to give yourself a few days, at least. Bonding with a Vampire is disorienting even when you mean to do it. And don't then immediately exhaust yourself."

I cringed. "So, you're not going to give me a lecture on letting Natalie bite me?"

"No. I mean, it's pretty obvious that Natalie had a fatal wound. I wish that you could have made this decision for your own reasons, not to save your friend, but I'm not going to scold you for saving her. Now, why don't we see about getting you out of here and getting some rest?"

"Yeah, rest sounds good."

Dear Reader,

Well, it wouldn't be the end of an Ember Academy book if I didn't leave you hanging, would it?

In all honesty, the events of this book and Book Six ended up flowing into each other in a way where there wasn't a clear breaking point.

But the next book will be the final book in the series, so there will be no cliffhangers, I promise.

If you've seen me talking about the next series that's going to be set at Ember Academy, you might not believe that, but I promise, that series is going to take place about ten years after the end of this one, and it's going to follow a completely new cast of characters.

Speaking of, I need to get back to writing.

See you next book!

Special Thanks

I just wanted to give a shout out to my Patreon supporters as well as everyone who has left reviews of my books!

My Patreon supporters are a massive help to me being able to do this as my job (or, well, one of them... Cue a joke about being a millennial in this economy while I cry over my two degrees...) and reviews are a massive help to me being able to do this emotionally. Seriously, they make my day and everyone who has left one deserves cookies!

Want to Keep in Touch?

If you want to connect with me and other fans of the series between books, I have a weekly newsletter where we discuss things like the best fantasy soundtracks to work to and which vampire lore is the best, and there's also a closed Facebook group where I talk about secret projects that aren't ready to be shown anywhere else just yet.

You can find all of these places at lcmawson.com/links

Other Series by L.C. Mawson

Snowverse
Ember Academy for Young Witches
lcmawson.com/emberacademy
Ember Academy for Magical Beings
lcmawson.com/ember-academy-for-magical-beings
Freya Snow – YA/NA Urban Fantasy
lcmawson.com/books/freyasnow
The Royal Cleaner – F/F Urban Fantasy
lcmawson.com/books/the-royal-cleaner
Engineered Rebel – Sci-fi/Urban Fantasy
lcmawson.com/engineered-rebel
Castaway Heart – Mermaid Romance (CW for Steamy Scenes and Domestic Violence)
lcmawson.com/castawayheart
Other
Aspects – YA Sci-fi
lcmawson.com/the-aspects
The Lady Ruth Constance Chapelstone Chronicles – Steampunk Novellas
lcmawson.com/books/ladyruth

Printed in Great Britain
by Amazon